Maigret and the Apparition

Georges Simenon

Maigret and the Apparition

Translated by Eileen Ellenbogen
Published in England under the title
Maigret and the Ghost

A Harvest Book
A Helen and Kurt Wolff Book
Harcourt Brace & Company
San Diego New York London

Library of Congress Cataloging-in-Publication Data
Simenon, Georges, 1903–1989.
Maigret and the apparition.
(A Harvest book)
Translation of Maigret et le fantôme.
"A Helen and Kurt Wolff book."
I. Title.
[PZ3.S5892Maega 1980] [PQ2637. I53]
843'.912   80-14124
ISBN 0-15-655127-6

Printed in the United States of America
K J I H G F

Maigret and the Apparition

1/ Inspector Lognon's Nocturnal Activities and His Wife's Infirmities

On the night in question, it was past one o'clock when the light went out in Maigret's office. The Chief Superintendent, his eyelids swollen with fatigue, opened the door communicating with the inspectors' room. Bonfils and young Lapointe were the officers on duty that night.

"Good night, boys," he mumbled.

Outside, the cleaning women were sweeping the vast lobby. He raised his hand in greeting. As always at this late hour, there was a draft, and the stairway was damp and freezing cold as he and Janvier went down together.

It was the middle of November. Rain had been falling all through the day. Maigret had not once set foot outside his overheated office since eight o'clock the previous morning, and before stepping out into the forecourt he turned up his coat collar.

"Can I give you a lift?"

A taxi, ordered by telephone, was waiting outside the main gate on the Quai des Orfèvres.

"Just as far as the nearest métro station, Chief."

The rain was coming down in sheets, and bouncing off the paving stones. The inspector got out at the Châtelet.

"Good night, Chief."

"Good night, Janvier."

They had parted like this hundreds of times before, with the same sense of somewhat jaded satisfaction.

A few minutes later Maigret, without making a sound, was creeping up the stairs to his apartment on Boulevard Richard Lenoir, groping in his pocket for the key, then turning it carefully in the lock. Almost immediately he heard Madame Maigret turning over in bed.

"Is that you?"

How often had he come home in the middle of the night to hear her call out these same words, her voice drugged with sleep, as she groped in the dark for the switch of the bedside lamp? Hundreds if not thousands of times. Then, in her nightdress, she would get out of bed and take a look at her husband, to see what sort of a mood he was in.

"Is it over?"

"Yes."

"Did the boy talk in the end?"

He nodded.

"Are you hungry? Would you like me to get you something?"

He hung his wet coat on the coat stand, and loosened his tie.

"Is there any beer in the refrigerator?"

On the way home, he had almost stopped the taxi in Place de la République, with the intention of going into one of the all-night brasseries and ordering some.

"Did it turn out as you expected?"

A dull case, if one can talk of dullness where the fate of three men is in the balance. One newspaper had man-

aged to introduce a hint of sensationalism with the head-
line THE MOTORCYCLE GANG.

On the first occasion, in broad daylight on Rue de
Rennes, two motorcycles had drawn in to the curb in
front of a jeweler's. The first motorcycle had been carrying two men; the second, one. The three men had tied
red scarves over their faces and gone into the shop. They
had emerged a few minutes later, carrying guns and a
quantity of jewelry and watches snatched from the display window and counter.

At first the crowd had been too stunned to react, but
when the first shock had subsided, a number of passers-by
in cars had driven off in pursuit of the thieves, causing
such a snarl in the process as to help, rather than hinder,
the escape of the wanted men.

"They'll try again," Maigret had predicted.

It had been a pretty meager haul, for the shop, owned
by a widow, stocked only very cheap stuff.

"This was by way of being a dress rehearsal."

It was the first time that motorcycles had been used
in a holdup.

The Chief Superintendent had guessed right, for, three
days later, the scene was re-enacted, only this time at a
luxury jeweler's on the Faubourg Saint-Honoré. The outcome was the same, except that on this occasion the
thieves got away with jewelry worth millions of old francs,
two hundred million, according to the newspapers, a
hundred million, according to the insurance-company as-
sessors.

However, one of the thieves had dropped his scarf
while escaping, and was arrested the following day at
his place of work, a locksmith's on Rue Saint-Paul.

By the evening of that same day, all three were under lock and key. The eldest of them was twenty-two years of age, and the youngest, Jean Bauche, nicknamed Jeannot, barely eighteen.

He was a tall, fair-haired youth, who wore his hair too long. He was also employed in the locksmith's workshop. His mother worked as a cleaning woman on Rue Saint-Antoine.

"Janvier and I have been taking turns all day," Maigret, looking glum, said to his wife.

Drinking beer and eating sandwiches the while.

" 'See here, Jeannot, you think you're tough, don't you? They talked you into believing you were. But it wasn't you or your two little friends who thought up either of those jobs. There's someone behind all this, someone who engineers things, while taking great care not to soil his own hands. He's only been out of Fresnes Prison two months, and he's none too keen to find himself back inside. You might as well admit it; he was in the vicinity in a stolen car, and he covered your retreat by a dazzling display of clumsy driving.' "

Maigret undressed, pausing from time to time to take a sip of beer. Disjointedly, he brought his wife up to date on the case.

"Those kids are as stubborn as they come. . . . They have their own peculiar code of honor. . . ."

He had ordered the arrest of three old ex-convicts, among them a man named Gaston Nouveau. As was only to be expected, he had a cast-iron alibi, having produced two witnesses ready to swear that at the time of the holdup he was in a bar on Avenue des Ternes.

There had been hours of fruitless interrogation. The eldest of the three motorcyclists, Victor Sidon, familiarly known as Granny because he was inclined to plumpness, kept darting sly glances at the Chief Superintendent. Saugier, nicknamed "Squib," wept and denied all knowledge of the affair.

"Janvier and I decided that our best course was to concentrate on young Bauche. We sent for his mother, who pleaded with him: " 'Talk, Jeannot! Can't you see that these gentlemen are not out to get you? They know perfectly well that you were led astray. . . .' "

Twenty hateful hours spent in leaning on a young boy, pushing him remorselessly to the limits of human endurance. It was not pleasant, either, to see him suddenly crack without warning.

" 'All right! I'll tell you everything. You were right; it was Nouveau who brought us together at the Lotus, and set up the job.' "

The Lotus was a small bar on Rue Saint-Antoine, much frequented by teen-agers, attracted by the music of the jukeboxes.

" 'And because of you, he'll have me beaten by his pals the minute I get out of prison. . . .' "

At last! The end of the day. Maigret, his head aching, got into bed.

"What time do you have to be at the office?"

"Nine."

"Couldn't you sleep late, just for once?"

"Wake me at eight."

As far as he was concerned, there had been no interval. He felt as if he had not slept at all. It seemed to him that he had no sooner shut his eyes than the doorbell rang, and his wife was creeping out of bed to answer it.

He could hear whispering in the entrance hall. The

voice seemed familiar, but he thought he must be dreaming, and buried his face in his pillow.

He could hear his wife's footsteps approaching the bed. Would she get back into bed? Had someone rung their doorbell by mistake? No. She touched him on the shoulder, and drew the curtains. Without having to open his eyes, he realized that it was daylight. Drowsily, he asked:

"What time is it?"

"Seven."

"Is there someone there?"

"It's Lapointe. He's waiting for you in the dining room."

"What does he want?"

"I don't know. Don't get out of bed yet. I'll bring you a cup of coffee."

Why did his wife sound as if she had just had some bad news? Why hadn't she given him a straight answer to a straight question. The sky was a dirty gray, and it was still raining.

Maigret's first guess was that Jean Bauche, realizing with terror all that he had admitted, had hanged himself in his cell at the Préfecture. Without waiting for his coffee, Maigret slipped on his trousers, ran a comb through his hair, and, still feeling fuddled, after having been waked from a deep sleep, went into the dining room.

Lapointe was standing at the window, wearing a black overcoat and carrying a black hat. After a night on duty, his chin was bristly.

Maigret looked at him inquiringly.

"I'm so sorry, Chief, to disturb your sleep only to bring you bad news. Something happened last night. . . . It concerns someone you're fond of. . . ."

"Janvier?"

"No . . . It's not one of our own men. . . ."

Madame Maigret came in, bearing two large cups of coffee.

"It's Lognon. . . ."

"Is he dead?"

"No, but he's very seriously hurt. He's been taken to Bichat for an emergency operation. One of their top surgeons, Mingault, has been at work on him for the past three hours. Knowing what a heavy day you had yesterday, I felt you needed your rest. That's why I didn't come earlier or phone. . . . Besides, at first they didn't think he had much chance of pulling through. . . ."

"What happened to him?"

"He was shot twice, in the stomach and just below the shoulder blade. . . ."

"Where did this happen?"

"On the sidewalk, on Avenue Junot."

"Was he alone?"

"Yes. For the time being, his colleagues in the Eighteenth Arrondissement are handling the case. . . ."

Maigret was drinking his coffee in small sips. He was not enjoying it as much as he usually did.

"I thought you'd probably want to be there when he regained consciousness. I've got a car waiting downstairs. . . ."

"Is anything more known about the incident?"

"Almost nothing. They don't even know what he was doing on Avenue Junot. A concierge nearby heard the shots, and called the police emergency number. A stray shot penetrated her shutters, shattering a windowpane and lodging in the wall above her bed. . . ."

"I'd better get dressed."

He went into the bathroom. Madame Maigret was laying out the breakfast, and Lapointe, having taken off his
coat, seated himself at the table.

Although Inspector Lognon, much as he had longed
to be, was not a member of the Crime Squad, nevertheless
Maigret and he had often worked together, almost every
time, in fact, that a sensational case had come up in the
Eighteenth Arrondissement. He was what is popularly
known as a "plain-clothes detective," one of twenty plain-
clothes inspectors with headquarters in the Town Hall
of Montmartre, on the corner of Rue Caulaincourt and
Rue du Mont-Cenis.

He was known to some as "Inspector Grumpy," because of his surly manner, but Maigret had nicknamed
him "Inspector Hapless," for it seemed to him that poor
Lognon had a positive gift for bringing upon himself
every kind of misfortune.

He was small and thin, and never without a head cold
from one year's end to the next, so that, in spite of being
probably the most abstemious man on the force, he
looked, with his red nose and watering eyes, the very picture of a drunkard.

He was afflicted with an ailing wife, who spent her
time trailing between her bed and an armchair near the
window, so that Lognon, when he went off duty, was
burdened with the housework, the shopping, and the
cooking. He could just about afford to pay a cleaning
woman to do the rooms once a week.

He had taken the competitive examination for admission to the Department of Criminal Investigation on four
separate occasions, and he had failed each time, through
some trivial slip or omission. And yet he was outstand-

ingly good at his job, a sort of bloodhound who, once he was on the scent, would never give up. He was stubborn and punctilious to a fault. He was one of those men who had only to pass a dubious character in the street to sense that something was amiss.

"Is there any hope of saving his life?"

"Apparently the doctors at Bichat think he has a thirty-percent chance."

As applied to a man who had earned the nickname Hapless, this was not very encouraging.

"Was he able to speak?"

Maigret, his wife, and Lapointe were eating the croissants that had just been delivered to the door by the baker's boy.

"No one in his section mentioned it, and I didn't want to press them for information."

Lognon was not the only one with an inferiority complex. Most of the district inspectors keep a wary eye on the Big House, as they call the Quai des Orfèvres, and when they are on to anything important that is likely to hit the headlines, they hate having it taken away from them.

"Let's go," sighed Maigret, putting on his coat, which was still damp from the previous night.

He caught a look in his wife's eye and knew that there was something she wanted to say to him. He guessed that she had just been struck with the same idea he had.

"Do you think you'll be in for lunch?"

"I very much doubt it."

"In that case, don't you think . . .?"

She was thinking of Madame Lognon, alone and helpless in her apartment.

"Hurry up and get dressed! We'll drop you at Place Constantin-Pecqueur.

The Lognons had lived there for the past twenty years, in a red-brick building with yellow-brick trim around every window. Maigret could not recall the number of the house.

Lapointe sat at the wheel of the little departmental car. Only twice in many years had Madame Maigret driven with her husband in one of these cars.

They drove past crowded buses. On the sidewalks, people were hurrying along, leaning forward and clutching their umbrellas, for fear they would be snatched away by the wind.

They reached Rue Caulaincourt, in Montmartre.

"This is it."

In the middle of the square stood a stone sculpture of a man and a woman. The woman was swathed in drapery, but for one exposed breast. On the side where it had been lashed by the rain, the figure was black.

"Give me a call at the office. I hope to be back there before lunch."

Having barely had time to complete one case, he was now embarked on another, about which he as yet knew nothing. He was fond of Lognon. Often, in his official reports, he had stressed his good qualities, and had even gone so far as to attribute to Lognon successes that were really his own. All to no avail. Poor old Inspector Hapless!

"Bichat Hospital first . . ."

A staircase. Corridors. Open doors, revealing rows of beds, from which rows of eyes stared at the two strangers as they went past.

They had been misdirected, and so were forced to re-

turn downstairs to the courtyard and go up another staircase, where at last they found, on guard outside a door
marked SURGICAL WING, an inspector from the Eighteenth
Arrondissement whom they knew. His name was Créac,
and there was an unlit cigarette between his lips.

"I think you'd be wise to put your pipe away, Chief
Superintendent. There's a real dragon in there, and she'll
come down on you like a ton of bricks, as she did on me
when I tried to light my cigarette. . . ."

Nurses were going to and fro, carrying enamel jugs
and bowls, and trays loaded with little bottles and nickel-
plated surgical instruments.

"Is he still in the operating room?"

The time was quarter to nine.

"They've been at work on him up there since four
o'clock this morning."

"Have you heard anything?"

"I went into that office over there on the left to inquire,
but the old bag . . ."

It was the matron's office, and the matron, according
to Créac, was a dragon. Maigret knocked at the door. An
unfriendly voice called out to him to come in.

"What do you want?"

"I'm sorry to disturb you, madame. I am the chief
superintendent in charge of the Crime Squad of the Department of Criminal Investigation. . . ."

Her frigid stare said "What of it?" as plainly as if she
had spoken aloud.

"I was wondering if you could tell me how the inspector is standing up to the operation."

"I shan't know until the operation is over. . . . All I
can say is that he is alive, seeing that the surgeon is still in
there. . . ."

"When he was brought in, was he able to talk?"

This time she looked at him with contempt, as if he had asked a stupid question.

"He'd lost more than half the blood in his body. He had to be given an emergency transfusion."

"How long before he regains consciousness, do you think?"

"You'll have to ask Professor Mingault."

"If you have a private room available, I'd be obliged if you would keep it for him. It's important. An inspector will be in attendance at his bedside. . . ."

Her attention was distracted by the opening of the door of the operating room. A man appeared in the passage, wearing a white cap and a bloodstained apron over his white overall.

"Professor, this person here is . . ."

"Chief Superintendent Maigret . . ."

"Pleased to meet you."

"Is he still alive?"

"For the moment . . . Unless there are unforeseen complications, I hope to be able to pull him through."

His forehead was running with perspiration, and his features were drawn with fatigue.

"Just one more thing . . . It's important to us that he should have a private room. . . ."

"See to that, please, Matron. . . . Now, if you'll excuse me . . ."

He strode off toward his office. Once again, the door opened. A surgical bed on wheels appeared, propelled by an orderly. Under the sheet could be traced the outline of a body, Lognon's body, stiff and seemingly drained of blood, with only the upper part of his face showing.

"Take him to Number 218, Bernard."

"Very well, Matron."

She walked behind the bed, with Maigret, Lapointe, and Créac close on her heels. It was a dismal procession, in the wan morning light coming from windows high above them. The sight of the straight rows of beds in the wards as they went past was scarcely cheering. It was like living through a bad dream.

A house surgeon emerged from the operating room and tagged on behind.

"Are you a member of his family?"

"No . . . I'm Chief Superintendent Maigret. . . ."

"Ah! So it is you!"

He looked at him searchingly, as if anxious to confirm that the Chief Superintendent really did look as he had imagined him to.

"The doctor says there's a chance that he may pull through. . . ."

It was a world apart, where voices lacked the resonance normal elsewhere, a world without echoes.

"If he said so . . ."

"Have you any idea how long it will be before he regains consciousness?"

Was Maigret's question so absurd that he deserved such a look as he got? The matron stopped the police officers at the door.

"No. Not now."

The wounded man had to be made comfortable and no doubt be given treatment, since nurses were wheeling in a variety of equipment, including an oxygen tent.

"You can wait out here, if you insist, but I'd rather you didn't. There are regular visiting hours."

Maigret glanced at his watch.

"I think I'd better be on my way, Créac. I'd like you

to be present, if possible, when he regains consciousness. If he's able to talk, take down verbatim everything he says."

He did not feel humiliated. No. All the same, he was a little ill at ease, not being accustomed to such disrespectful treatment. With these people, whose attitude toward life and death was different from that of the ordinary man, his reputation cut no ice.

It was a relief, outside in the forecourt, to be able to light his pipe. Lapointe, at the same time, took the opportunity to light a cigarette.

"As for you, you'd better go home to bed, after you've dropped me at the Town Hall in the Eighteenth Arrondissement."

"Would you mind very much if I stayed with you, Chief?"

"You were up all night. . . ."

"Oh, well, you know, at my age . . ."

The Town Hall was no distance away. In the inspectors' duty room, there were three plain-clothes detectives engaged in writing reports. Crouching over their typewriters, they looked thoroughly conscientious.

"Good morning, gentlemen . . . Which of you knows the facts?"

He knew the men, if not by name, at least by sight, and all three had stood up as he came into the room.

"All of us, and none of us . . ."

"Did anyone go to break the news to Madame Lognon?"

"Durantel went."

There were damp footprints on the wooden floor, and a lingering smell of tobacco smoke about the place.

"Was Lognon on to something?"

They looked at him, hesitating. At last, one of the three, a small fat man, began:

"That's just the question we've been asking ourselves. . . . You know Lognon, Chief Superintendent. . . . He had a way of making a mystery of it when he was on the trail of something. . . . Often, he would work for weeks on a case before saying a word about it to any of us. . . ."

And no wonder, considering the number of times others had been given the credit for his achievements!

"He's been very secretive for the past fortnight at least. And sometimes, when he came into the office, he looked as if he was working up to something big, which he intended to spring on us as a terrific surprise."

"Did he drop any hints?"

"No. But he had himself transferred more or less permanently to night duty. . . ."

"Do you know where he spent his time?"

"He was seen once or twice by the night patrols on Avenue Junot, not far from the spot where he was attacked. . . . But not recently . . . He used to leave here about nine at night, and wouldn't get back until three or four in the morning. Sometimes he would be out all night. . . ."

"Didn't he put in any reports?"

"I've looked in the register. He just wrote 'Nothing to report.' "

"Have you any men at the scene of the shooting?"

"Three. Chinquier is in charge."

"What about the press?"

"It's not easy to hush up an attempt on the life of a detective inspector. . . . Would you like a word with the superintendent?"

"Not just now."

With Lapointe still at the wheel, Maigret had himself driven to Avenue Junot. The last of the autumn leaves were falling from the trees and sticking to the wet pavements. The rain, which was still pelting down, had not deterred a crowd of about fifty people from gathering in the middle of the road.

A square section of the pavement had been cordoned off, and there were uniformed policemen on guard. When Maigret got out of the car to thread his way among spectators and umbrellas, cameras clicked all around him.

"Just one more, Chief Superintendent . . . Could you move forward a little?"

He glared at them as balefully as the matron had glared at him in the hospital. On the small stretch of pavement protected from trampling feet, the rain had not entirely washed out the bloodstains, though they were gradually being diluted, and, since it had not been possible to use chalk, the position of the fallen body had been outlined with twigs.

Inspector Deliot, yet another member of the Eighteenth Arrondissement Division, removed his sopping hat in deference to Maigret.

"Chinquier is inside, talking to the concierge, Chief Superintendent. He was the first of us to arrive on the scene."

The building was fairly old, but very clean and well maintained. The Chief Superintendent went in and pushed open the glass door of the lodge, just in time to see Inspector Chinquier putting his notebook back in his pocket.

"I was expecting you. I was surprised to find no one here from the Quai."

"I went to the hospital first."

"How did the operation go?"

"Quite successfully, I gather. The doctor thinks he may pull through."

The lodge was clean and neat. The concierge, about forty-five, was still an attractive woman, with a pleasing figure.

"Please sit down, gentlemen. . . . I've just been telling the inspector everything I know. . . . Look over here, on the floor. . . ."

The green linoleum was strewn with slivers of glass from a broken windowpane.

"And here . . ."

She pointed to a hole about three feet above the bed, which stood at the far end of the room.

"Were you alone in here?"

"Yes. My husband is night porter at the Palace Hotel, on Avenue des Champs-Elysées. He doesn't get back here until eight in the morning."

"Where is he now?"

"In the kitchen."

She pointed to a closed door.

"He's trying to get some rest, because, in spite of everything, he'll have to go on duty tonight as usual."

"I am taking it for granted, Chinquier, that you have asked all the necessary questions. So don't be offended if I ask a few questions of my own."

"Will you be needing me?"

"Not for the moment."

"In that case, if you don't mind, I'll take a look around upstairs."

Maigret frowned, wondering what the inspector had in mind to do up there, but he didn't pursue the point for fear of causing offense to the local man.

"I'm sorry to have to bother you, madame. . . ."

"Madame Sauget. The tenants all call me Angèle."

"Do please sit down."

"I'm so used to standing!"

She drew the curtain across the bed. It was usually kept closed up during the day, thus turning the main area into a small sitting room.

"Can I get you anything? A cup of coffee?"

"Thank you, no. So, last night, after you went to bed . . ."

"Yes, I heard a voice call out:

" 'Please release the catch.' "

"Did you notice the time?"

"My alarm clock has a luminous dial. It was half past two."

"Was it one of the tenants asking to be let out?"

"No. It was that gentleman. . . ."

She looked embarrassed, as if she felt she had been trapped into committing an indiscretion.

"What gentleman?"

"The man who was shot at . . ."

Maigret and Lapointe exchanged bewildered glances.

"Inspector Lognon, do you mean?"

She nodded, and went on:

"One shouldn't keep anything back from the police, should one? I'm not one to gossip about my tenants, as a rule. I never talk about their comings and goings, or the company they keep. Their private lives are no concern of mine. But after what has happened . . ."

"Have you known the inspector long?"

"Yes, for years . . . Ever since my husband and I came here to live . . . But I didn't know his name. . . . I used to see him go past, and I knew he was a police officer, because he came into the lodge a few times on identity checks. He never said much. . . ."

"When did you get to know him better?"

"When he started coming in to call on the young lady on the fourth floor."

This time Maigret was struck speechless. As for Lapointe, he looked as if he had been hit over the head. Not all policemen are necessarily saints. Maigret knew that there were men in his own section who were not above indulging in extramarital adventures.

But Lognon! He just could not imagine old Hapless slinking out at night to visit a young woman in a building barely two hundred yards from his own apartment.

"You're quite sure we're talking about the same man?"

"He's not the sort you'd forget in a hurry, is he?"

"How long has he been in the habit of . . . calling on the lady?"

"About ten days."

"I take it, then, that the first evening, he came in with her?"

"Yes."

"Did he try to hide his face as he went past the lodge?"

"That was the impression I got."

"Did he come back often."

"Almost every night."

"Was it very late when he left?"

"At the beginning—that's to say the first three or four nights—he left about midnight. After that he stayed longer, until two or three in the morning."

"What is this woman's name?"

"Marinette . . . Marinette Augier . . . She's a very pretty girl. She's about twenty-five, and ladylike in her manners."

"Was she in the habit of entertaining men?"

"I think I can answer that with a clear conscience, because she never made any secret of her private life. . . . For a whole year, a handsome young man used to visit her two or three times a week. She told me they were engaged. . . ."

"Used to spend the night with her?"

"You're bound to find out in the end. . . . Yes . . After he stopped coming, she looked sad, I thought. . . . One morning, when she called in to collect her mail, I asked her if the engagement was broken off, and she said:

" 'You're a good soul, Angèle, but I don't want to talk about it. It's no good upsetting oneself over a man. They just aren't worth it.'

"She must have succeeded in putting him out of her mind, because not long afterward she was her old, cheerful self again. . . . She's a very lively girl, and bursting with health."

"What does she do for a living?"

"She's a cosmetician, so she tells me. She works in a beauty salon on Avenue Matignon. . . . That probably explains why she is always so well groomed and tastefully dressed. . . ."

"What about her boyfriend?"

"The fiancé who stopped coming? He was in his thirties. I don't know what his occupation was. I don't even know his surname. I always called him 'Monsieur Henri,' because that was how he announced himself, when he went past the lodge at night."

"When was the relationship broken off?"

"Last winter, around Christmas."

"Which means that for nearly a year this young woman—what's her name? Marinette? . . ."

"Marinette Augier."

"Are you, then, saying that for the best part of a year she has had no one up there with her?"

"Except for an occasional visit from her brother. He lives in the suburbs somewhere, and he's married and has three children."

"And about a fortnight ago, she came home one evening in the company of Inspector Lognon?"

"As I have already told you."

"And since then, he's been here every night?"

"Except Sundays, unless he managed to slip in and out without my seeing him."

"Did he never come during the day?"

"No, but I've just thought of something. One evening, when he arrived as usual at nine o'clock, I ran after him as he was starting to go upstairs, and called out:

" 'Marinette isn't in!'

" 'I know,' he said. 'She's at her brother's.'

"But he went on up just the same, without explanation, which, now I think of it, suggests that she had lent him her key."

Maigret now understood why Inspector Chinquier had gone up there.

"Is your tenant in her apartment now?"

"No."

"Has she gone to work?"

"I don't know, but when I went up to break the news to her as gently as I could . . ."

"What time was this?"

"After I had telephoned for the police . . ."

"In other words, about three in the morning?"

"Yes . . . I thought she couldn't have failed to hear the shots. All the other tenants did. Some were leaning out

of their windows. Others were coming down the stairs in
their dressing gowns, to find out what was going on. . . .

"It wasn't a pretty sight, what was out there in the
street. . . . So I ran upstairs and knocked at her door.
There was no answer. . . . I went in, and found the apartment empty. . . ."

She gave the Chief Superintendent a somewhat smug
look, as if to say:

"I daresay you've come across a good many peculiar
things in the course of your career, but I defy you to cap
this!"

She was right. All Maigret and Lapointe could do was
to gape blankly at one another. Maigret thought of his
wife, who, at this very moment, was with Madame Lognon, whose Christian name was Solange, offering conso-
lation, and doubtless doing all the housework for her!

"Could she have left the building at the same time as
he did?"

"I'm sure she didn't. I have very sharp ears, and I'm
certain only one person went out, and that was a man."

"Did he call out his name as he went past?"

"No. He was in the habit of simply saying:

" 'Fourth floor.'

"I recognized his voice. And besides, he was the only
one to announce himself in that way."

"Could she have gone out before he arrived?"

"No. I only once released the catch last night, at
eleven-thirty, to let in the third-floor tenants, who had
been to see a movie."

"So she must have gone out after the shots were fired?"

"It's the only possible explanation. As soon as I saw
the body lying on the pavement, I rushed back here to
call police emergency. . . . I was reluctant to shut the

front door. I couldn't. . . . I would have felt I was deserting the poor man. . . ."

"Did you bend over him, to see if he was dead?"

"It was dreadful. . . . I have a horror of blood, but I did."

"Was he conscious?"

"I don't know. . . ."

"Did he say anything?"

"His lips were moving. . . . I could see he was trying to speak. . . . I thought I caught just one word, but I must have been mistaken, because it doesn't make sense. . . . Maybe he was delirious."

"What was the word?"

"Apparition."

She flushed, obviously afraid that the Chief Superintendent and the inspector would laugh at her, or accuse her of fantasizing.

$\mathbf{2}$ / Lunch at Chez Manière

One might have been forgiven for thinking that the man had chosen this particular moment in order to create the maximum dramatic effect. Had he, perhaps, been listening at the door? Scarcely had the word "apparition" been spoken when the doorknob was seen to turn, the door to open a crack, and a head without a body to appear through the gap.

The face was pale, the features indeterminate, the eyelids and mouth drooping. It took Maigret a second or two to realize that the man's lugubrious expression was largely due to the absence of dentures.

"Why aren't you asleep, Raoul?"

And, as if they didn't know, she introduced him:

"My husband, Chief Superintendent."

He was much older than she, and was wearing a hideous purple dressing gown over crumpled pajamas.

In his gold-braided uniform, behind his desk at the Palace Hotel, he might pass muster, but here and now, unshaven, his body slumped, and wearing the peevish look of one who has been deprived of sleep, he seemed both ludicrous and pathetic.

With a cup of coffee in his hand, he acknowledged Maigret's presence with a vague nod, and then turned his gaze toward the lace window curtains, beyond which could be seen a mass of dark shapes, gathered together in the still-persistent rain, in spite of the efforts of the uniformed policemen to hold them back.

"How long is this going on?" he groaned.

Sleep, which he needed and had a right to, was being denied him, and, to look at him, one might have supposed that he was the true victim in the case.

"Why don't you take one of those pills the doctor prescribed?"

"They give me stomach-ache."

He retired into a corner, sat down, and began drinking his coffee, his slipper dangling from one bare foot. During the remainder of the interview, he never once opened his mouth, except to emit a sigh.

"I'd be grateful, madame, if you would try to remember in detail exactly what happened from the time when you were asked to release the catch."

Why such an attractive woman should have married a man at least twenty years older than herself was no concern of Maigret's. Presumably, at that time she had never seen him without his dentures.

"I heard someone call out:

" 'Please release the catch.'

"And then the same voice, which I knew well, added:

" 'Fourth floor!'

"As I have already told you, I looked at the clock automatically. It is a habit with me. It was half past two. I put out my hand to press the button. There's no cord to pull nowadays, as there used to be, just an electrically operated catch.

"It was just then that I thought I heard a car engine, as if a car had drawn up, not in front of this building but the one next door, leaving the engine running. I actually thought it was the Hardsins, who live next door, and often get home very late.

"It all happened so quickly, you see. I heard Monsieur Lognon's footsteps in the hall. Then the door banged. Immediately after that the engine revved up, the car moved off, and three shots were fired, one after the other. . . .

"The third shot seemed to go off right inside the lodge itself, what with the shock of the impact on the shutter, the shattering of the glass, and the strange noise above my head. . . ."

"What happened to the car? Did it drive on? You're sure there was a car?"

The husband, with lowered head, looked at each of them in turn, while at the same time absently stirring his coffee.

"I'm quite sure. The street is on a slope. To go up it, cars have to accelerate. That particular car roared away at full tilt, in the direction of Rue Norvins. . . ."

"Do you remember hearing anyone cry out?"

"No. At first, I was so scared I couldn't move. But you know what we women are. We just have to know, to find out what's going on. I switched on the light, grabbed my dressing gown, and rushed out into the hall."

"Was the street door shut?"

"I told you, I heard it slam. I pressed my ear against it, but I could hear nothing but the rain. Then I opened it a crack, and saw the body lying barely six feet away."

"What way was it facing? Up or down the steet?"

"It looked as if he'd been making for Rue Caulaincourt. The poor soul was clutching his stomach with both hands, and his fingers were dripping with blood. His eyes were open, and he stared at me fixedly."

"And you went out and bent over him, and it was then that you heard or thought you heard the word 'apparition.' Is that right?"

"I could swear that was what he said. Windows were flung open. There are no private telephones in the apartments. All the tenants have to use the one in the lodge. Two of them have been on the waiting list for a phone of their own for over a year.

"I went indoors and looked up the police emergency number in the telephone book. One ought to carry a number like that in one's head, but one doesn't think of these things, especially in a respectable place like this. . . ."

"Was there a light on in the hall?"

"No. Only in my lodge. The policeman asked me several questions, to satisfy himself that it wasn't a hoax, so that it took some time. . . ."

The telephone was fixed to the wall. Anyone using it would not be able to see out into the hall.

"Some of the tenants had come downstairs. . . . But I've told you all that. . . . It wasn't until I had replaced the receiver that I thought of Marinette, and rushed up to the fourth floor. . . ."

"I'm much obliged to you. I wonder if I might use your telephone?"

Maigret called headquarters.

"Hello! Is that you, Lucas? . . . I daresay you've seen Lapointe's note about Lognon? . . . No, I'm not calling from the hospital. . . . They can't say for sure yet whether he's going to pull through. . . . I'm on Avenue Junot. . . .

I want you to go to Bichat. . . . Yes, in person, if you
can manage it . . . You'd better pull rank for all you're
worth, because the people there haven't much time for
interlopers.

"Try to have a word with the house surgeon who was
present during the operation. I don't suppose Professor
Mingault will be available at this hour. . . . I presume
they've extracted at least one bullet, if not both. . . . Yes
. . . I'd like to have as many details as possible, in advance
of the official report. . . . As to the bullets, you'd better
get them straight off to the lab. . . ."

Formerly, this sort of work was done by an outside
consultant, a man named Gastienne-Renette, but the
Department of Criminal Investigation now had their own
ballistics expert in the Forensic Laboratory, up in the
attics of the Palais de Justice.

"I'll be seeing you later this morning or in the early
afternoon. . . ."

The Chief Superintendent turned to Lapointe.

"Don't you think you really ought to go home to bed?"

"I don't feel in the least sleepy, Chief. . . ."

The night porter of the Palace Hotel gave him a look
of mingled envy and reproof.

"In that case, off with you to Avenue Matignon. It
shouldn't be too difficult to locate the beauty salon where
Marinette Augier works. There's can't be all that many
of them. . . . I shouldn't think there's much hope of finding her there. . . . Try to find out all you can about her."

"Very well, Chief."

"As for me, I'm going upstairs. . . ."

Maigret was a little annoyed with himself for not having thought of the bullets earlier, when he was actually
at the hospital. But this was not just any ordinary case.

Somehow, because it concerned Lognon, it had assumed the character almost of a private investigation.

While he was there, his thoughts were almost wholly occupied with the inspector, and he had allowed himself to be overawed by the matron, the doctor, and the wards full of rows of watching patients.

There was no elevator in the building on Avenue Junot. There was no stair carpet either, but the wooden treads, worn smooth by use, were well polished, and the banisters gleamed. There were two apartments to each floor, and beside some of the doors brass plates could be seen, inscribed with the names of the tenants.

When he reached the fourth floor, he found the door ajar. He pushed it open and crossed a rather dark entrance hall leading to a living room, where he found Inspector Chinquier smoking a cigarette in an armchair covered with flowered chintz.

"I've been expecting you. . . . Has she told you all about it?"

"Yes."

"Did she mention the car? . . . That's what struck me the most. . . . Take a look at this. . . ."

He stood up and took from his pocket three shining spent cartridges, which he had wrapped in a scrap of newspaper.

"We found these in the road. . . . If the shots were fired from a moving car, as seems likely, then the man who fired them must have held his arm out through the window. . . . As you will have noticed, they're .763's."

Chinquier was a conscientious police officer, and knew his job.

"The weapon was probably a Mauser automatic—a heavy gun, that—which couldn't be slipped into a handbag or a trouser pocket. . . . Do you see what I'm getting at? Everything points to a pro, and he must have had at least one accomplice, because he couldn't possibly drive and aim at the same time. A jealous lover wouldn't be likely to rope in a pal to help him get rid of a rival. . . . And besides, Lognon was shot in the stomach."

A marksman would indeed stand a better chance by aiming at the stomach rather than the chest, for the victim seldom recovers with his intestines perforated in a dozen places by a large-caliber bullet.

"Have you been round the apartment?"

"I'd be glad if you would have a look round yourself."

There was another aspect of this case that made Maigret uneasy. It was the local inspectors themselves who had handled it in its early stages. They might not have thought much of Lognon when he was able to stand on his own two feet, but he was still their colleague, and now the victim of attempted murder. In such circumstances, the Chief Superintendent could scarcely elbow them out of the way and take charge himself.

"Quite a pleasant room, don't you think?"

On a bright day, no doubt, it would be even pleasanter. The walls were painted a bright yellow; the floor was highly polished and spread with a paler yellow carpet. The furniture, more or less contemporary in design, was tastefully chosen. The room, which served as both a sitting room and a dining room, was equipped with every comfort, including a television set and a record player.

The first thing Maigret had noticed on coming in was the table in the center of the room, on which stood an electric percolator, a cup with a little coffee left in it, a sugar bowl, and a bottle of brandy.

"Only one cup," he mumbled. "You haven't touched

it, have you, Chinquier? You'd better call the Quai and
ask them to send along some of the forensic fellows. . . ."

He had not taken off his coat, and he now put his hat
back on his head. One of the armchairs was turned to
face the window, and beside it stood a small occasional
table, with an ashtray containing seven or eight cigarette
stubs.

There were two doors opening off the living room. One
led into the kitchen, which was clean and neat, and
looked more like an Ideal Homes setup than the sort of
kitchen usually to be found in old buildings in Paris.

The other door opened into the bedroom. The bed was
unmade. The pillow, the only pillow, still showed the
dent where a head had lain.

A pale-blue dressing gown was carelessly thrown over
the back of a chair, the jacket of a matching pair of
women's pajamas lay in a heap on the floor, and the
trousers were against the wardrobe.

Chinquier was back already.

"I've had a word with Moers on the phone. His men
are on their way. Have you had time to look around?
Have you seen inside the wardrobe?"

"Not yet . . ."

He opened it. There were five dresses on hangers, a
fur-trimmed winter coat, and two tailored suits, one
beige, the other navy.

There were suitcases stacked in a row on the top shelf.

"Do you see what I'm getting at? It doesn't look as if
she's taken any luggage with her. And if you look in the
chest of drawers, you'll find all her underwear tidily
folded away."

From the window could be seen quite an extensive
view of Paris, but today in particular the gray sky, drip-

ping rain, dominated the buildings. Beyond the bed was
a door leading to a bathroom. Nothing was missing there
either, not even a toothbrush or any beauty preparations.

If the apartment was anything to go by, Marinette
Augier was a home-loving girl, with excellent taste and
a liking for her creature comforts.

"I forgot to ask the concierge whether she did her own
cooking, or went out for her meals," admitted Maigret.

"I asked about that. She almost always had her meals
here. . . ."

The refrigerator contained, among other things, half a
cold chicken, a quantity of butter and cheese, some fruit,
two bottles of beer and one of mineral water. There was
another bottle, opened, on the bedside table.

But of greater interest to the Chief Superintendent was
an ashtray, also on the bedside table, containing two
cigarette stubs stained with lipstick.

"She smoked American cigarettes. . . ."

"Whereas the stubs in the living room are all Caporals.
Is that what you're getting at?"

The two men exchanged glances. They had both been
struck with the same thought.

"If the state of the bed means anything, it couldn't
have been used for any amorous frolics last night."

In spite of the tragic circumstances, Maigret had difficulty in suppressing a smile at the thought of Inspector
Grumpy in a clinch with a lovely young beauty consultant.

Had they quarreled? Had Lognon stumped off into the
other room to sulk and chain-smoke, leaving his mistress
alone in bed?

There was something that didn't quite ring true in all
this, and, once again, Maigret was reminded that from

the beginning he had not approached the problem with his usual clearheadedness.

"I'm sorry to have to ask you to go downstairs again, Chinquier, but there's just one thing I forgot to ask the concierge. Could you find out whether, when she came up here, she found the light on in the living room?"

"I can tell you that. The bedroom door was open, and there was a light on in there, but the rest of the apartment was in darkness."

Together, they went back into the living room, with its two French windows opening onto a balcony which ran around the building, a common feature of the top stories of so many old buildings in Paris.

In spite of the overcast sky, it was just possible to see, in misty outline, the Eiffel Tower above the gleaming wet slates of hundreds of rooftops, with a smoking chimney here and there.

Maigret remembered Avenue Junot as it had been at the start of his career. It had scarcely been an avenue then, with only a few buildings in multiple occupation, interspersed with gardens and patches of waste ground. The first person to build a private house there had been a painter, and daringly modern it had seemed at the time!

Others followed his lead, among them a novelist and an opera singer, and before long Avenue Junot had developed into a fashionable address.

Standing at the French windows, the Chief Superintendent looked down, and observed that many of the houses below were squeezed right up against each other. The one opposite, judging from the architecture, must have been about fifteen years old. It had three floors.

Was it the home of a painter? The top floor, almost

entirely glass, seemed to suggest it. Dark curtains had
been drawn across the picture windows, leaving a gap
of no more than eighteen inches.

If anyone had asked the Chief Superintendent what
he was thinking about, he would have been hard put to
it to reply. He was simply registering impressions. Hap-
hazardly, as they struck him. At times he stared out the
windows, at other times he roamed about the apartment.
Sooner or later, he knew, all these impressions would
coalesce and become meaningful.

He could hear sounds, traffic in the streets, heavy footsteps on the stairs, voices, banging. The team from the
Forensic Laboratory had arrived with its equipment,
led by Moers, who had taken the trouble to come in
person.

"Where's the body?" he asked, his blue eyes, as usual,
looking a little puzzled behind the thick lenses of his
spectacles.

"There is no body. Hasn't Chinquier put you in the
picture?"

"I didn't want to waste time," explained the local inspector apologetically.

"It concerns Lognon. He was shot just as he was leaving this building. . . ."

"Is he dead?"

"He's been taken to Bichat Hospital. There's just a
chance that he may pull through. He spent part of last
night in this apartment with a woman. I'd very much like
to know whether he left any prints in the bedroom, besides those you will find in here. Fingerprint everything
you can. Are you coming down with me, Chinquier?"

He waited until they were in the hall on the ground
floor to murmur softly:

"It might be as well to find out what the other tenants and the neighbors have to say. It's not very likely that any of them were leaning out of their windows when the shots were fired. Not in this weather. But you never can tell.

"The girl, Marinette, may have taken a taxi, in which case it shouldn't be too difficult to trace the driver. She probably went down the street toward Place Constantin-Pecqueur, where there are more taxis than there are at the top of the hill. . . . You and your colleagues know the district better than I do. . . ."

Shaking Chinquier by the hand, he sighed.

"The best of luck to you!"

And he pushed open the glass door of the lodge. The husband, it seemed, had at last decided to go to bed, judging from the sound of steady breathing coming from behind the curtain.

"Is there anything more I can do to help?" murmured Angèle Sauget.

"No. I want to make a phone call, but I won't do it from here. I don't want to disturb his sleep."

"You mustn't think too badly of him. When he doesn't get his regular hours of sleep, he's impossible. I've given him a sleeping pill, and it's just started to work."

"If anything comes back to you that you have forgotten to tell me, be sure to call me at the Quai des Orfèvres."

"I doubt if anything will, but if it does, I promise I'll let you know. If only those wretched reporters and photographers would go away! They're the ones that are drawing the crowds."

"I'll see if I can get them to move farther off."

As was only to be expected, in spite of the attempts

of the policemen to hold them back, they mobbed him the minute he set foot outside the door.

"May I have your attention, gentlemen! At this stage of the case, I know no more than you do. Inspector Lognon was attacked by persons unknown, in the execution of his duty. . . ."

"Duty?" someone called out, waggishly.

"I said in the execution of his duty, and I repeat it. He was gravely wounded, and has been operated on by Professor Mingault at Bichat Hospital. However, he is not likely to be in any condition to talk for some hours, possibly even for some days.

"Until that time, there is no point in speculating. In any case, there is nothing more to see here. However, if you care to call at the Quai des Orfèvres this afternoon, I may have further news for you. . . ."

"What was the inspector doing inside the building? Is it true that a young woman has disappeared?"

"See you this afternoon!"

"Have you nothing more to say?"

"I've told you all I know."

With his collar turned up and his hands in his pockets, he plodded away down the avenue. Two or three clicks told him that, for want of a better subject, they were photographing him from behind, and, when he looked back, the reporters were beginning to disperse.

When he reached Rue Caulaincourt, he went into the first bistro he came to, and, because he felt a little chilly, ordered a hot toddy.

"Would you be so good as to let me have three telephone *jetons*?"

"Did you say three?"

He gulped down a generous mouthful of his toddy

before going into the telephone booth. His first call was to the hospital. As he had expected, he was switched from one extension to another before being connected with the matron of the surgical wing.

"No, he's not dead. One of our house physicians is with him at present, and one of your inspectors is waiting outside in the corridor. There is still no firm prognosis. Ah! Here's another of your men just coming into my office. . . ."

Resignedly, he hung up, and dialed the headquarters number.

"Has Lapointe come in yet?"

"He's been trying to reach you at Avenue Junot. I'll put him on for you."

Through the glass panes of the booth Maigret could see the zinc counter, and the proprietor in his shirt sleeves pouring two large glasses of red wine for a couple of workmen.

"Are you there, Chief? I had no difficulty in finding the beauty salon, since it's the only one on Avenue Matignon. It's very luxurious. Apparently, there's a man working there by the name of Marcellin, whom all the ladies speak of with bated breath. . . . Marinette Augier didn't come in to work today, which surprised her colleagues, because she is usually so very punctual and conscientious. . . .

"She never confided in anyone about her relationship with the inspector. . . . She has a married brother, who lives in Vanves, but they don't know his address. He works for an insurance company, and Marinette sometimes used to phone him at his office. The firm is the Fraternal Assurance. . . . I looked it up in the telephone book. It has offices in Rue Le Peletier. . . .

"I thought I ought to ask you before going there. . . ."

"Is Janvier there?"

"He's busy typing a report."

"Ask him if it's urgent. I'm most anxious that you should get some rest, so that you'll be fresh when I need you. . . ."

A brief silence at the end of the line. Then Lapointe's voice, sounding resigned:

"He says it's not urgent."

"In that case, put him in the picture, will you? I want him to go to Rue Le Peletier and see if he can get a lead on where Marinette might be hiding herself. . . ."

The little café was filling up, mostly with regulars. They were served with their usual drinks, without having to order. Several of the customers had recognized him and were darting inquisitive glances toward the glassed-in phone booth.

He had to look up Lognon's number. As he had expected, it was Madame Maigret who answered.

"Where are you?" she asked.

"Shh! . . . For heaven's sake, don't tell her that I'm within a few yards of her apartment. How is she?"

His wife hesitated. He could guess why.

"I suppose she's in bed, and feeling worse than her husband?"

"Yes."

"Have you got a meal ready for her?"

"I had to go out and do some shopping first."

"So she can be left?"

"Not if she can help it!"

"Whether she likes it or not, tell her I need you here, and meet me as soon as you can at Chez Manière."

"Are you inviting me out to lunch?"

She could scarcely believe her ears. They did occasionally go out for dinner on a weekend, but hardly ever for lunch, and certainly not when he was busy on a case.

The Chief Superintendent, returning to the bar to finish his drink, noticed that the spontaneity had gone out of the voices around him. This was the price of all the publicity foisted on him by the press, which was so often a handicap in his work.

Someone, avoiding his eye, said:

"Is it true that old Grumpy has been shot by gangsters?"

Another voice, deliberately trying to sound mysterious, replied:

"If it really was gangsters."

So, rumors were already rife in the district regarding the inspector's relationship with Marinette. Maigret paid for his drink and, with all eyes upon him, went out of the bistro and made his way to Chez Manière.

It was a brasserie, adjacent to a flight of stone steps. It had once been a popular haunt of local celebrities, and was still patronized by actresses, writers, and painters. It was too early for the regulars to show up. Most of the tables were vacant, and there were not more than four or five customers leaning on the bar.

He took off his wet coat and hat, and collapsed with a sigh of relief onto the bench nearest the window.

Looking about him dreamily, he lit his pipe, and had smoked it almost to the end when he spotted Madame Maigret, holding her umbrella like a shield, in the act of crossing the street.

"It feels so strange, meeting you like this. . . . It must be at least fifteen years since we were here last. . . . It was one evening after the theater. Do you remember?"

"Yes . . . What will you have?"

He handed her the menu.

"I don't need to ask what you're going to have. It will be the *andouillette*, I'm sure. . . . I wonder if I might venture to let myself go, and have lobster mayonnaise?"

They sat in silence until the hors d'oeuvre and a bottle of Loire wine were brought to the table. The atmosphere was intimate, with the windows misted and the tables around them empty.

"I feel almost as if I were one of your colleagues. . . . When you called to say you wouldn't be home for lunch, I could picture you eating in a place like this with Lucas or Janvier."

"It's just as likely that I would have stayed in my office, and had sandwiches and a glass of beer. . . . Tell me all about it. . . ."

"I don't want to sound catty. . . ."

"Just be your own truthful self."

"You've often spoken to me about her and her husband. He was always the one you were sorry for, and I've sometimes wondered whether you weren't being a little unfair. . . ."

"And now?"

"I'm not as sorry for her as I was, though I daresay she can't help herself. . . . I found her in bed, attended by the concierge and a neighbor, an old woman who never stops fiddling with the beads of her rosary. They had sent for the doctor because, to look at her, you'd have thought she was dying. . . ."

"Was she surprised to see you?"

"You'll never guess what her first words to me were! She said:

" 'Well, now at any rate, your husband will have to stop persecuting him. I daresay, by this time, he's sorry he obstructed Charles's promotion to a job at headquarters.'

"At first, I felt very uncomfortable. . . . And then, quite by chance, the doctor called. He's small, elderly, and placid, and he has a mischievous twinkle in his eye. . . .

"The concierge returned to her lodge. The old lady, still fidgeting with her beads, followed me into the dining room.

" 'Poor soul!' she said. 'What sorry, weak creatures we are, when it comes down to it! When one thinks of all that is going on around us, one is almost afraid to set foot outside one's own door.'

"I asked her how serious Madame Lognon's illness was, and she said that her legs were so weak that she could scarcely stand. It was something to do with her bones, she thought."

They couldn't help exchanging smiles. The contrast between lunching at home on Avenue Richard Lenoir and in the intimate atmosphere of the little restaurant struck them both at the same time. Madame Maigret especially was tremendously thrilled by it. Her eyes sparkled and her color rose as she spoke.

When lunching or dining at home, it was usually Maigret who did all the talking, since she had little of interest to relate. On this occasion, she was relishing the opportunity of being useful to him.

"Is all this really of interest to you?"

"Very much so. Go on."

"After he had finished examining her, the doctor beckoned to me to follow him to the entrance hall, and we stood there talking in whispers. He began by asking me if I really was the wife of Chief Superintendent Maigret. He seemed very surprised to find me there.

"I explained. . . . Well you can guess what I said to him. . . .

" 'I understand how you feel,' he mumbled. 'It's most generous of you. . . . But allow me to give you a word of warning. . . . While I don't claim that she has the constitution of an ox, I can assure you that she is very far from being seriously ill. . . . I have attended her for ten years. . . . And I'm not the only one!

" 'She is forever calling in one or another of my professional colleagues, hoping against hope that one of them will find something seriously wrong with her. But, whenever I dare suggest that she should consult a psychiatrist or a neurologist, she grows indignant, and says she is not mad, and that I don't know the rudiments of my job. . . .

" 'Perhaps her marriage has not turned out as she had hoped. At any rate, there is no doubt that she is deeply resentful of the fact that her husband has not made more progress in his career.

" 'And, by way of revenge, she plays the helpless invalid, to force him to attend to all her needs, do the housework, and, in general, lead a life that, by any standards, is intolerable. . . .

" 'You came to see her this morning. All well and good. But if you show yourself too willing, she'll latch on to you with all her strength. . . .

" 'I telephoned Bichat in her presence, and I was able to assure her that her husband's chances of recovery were excellent. . . . I laid it on a bit thick. . . . But it made no difference. . . . She had no sympathy to spare for her husband, only for herself. . . .' "

The *andouillette*, with fried potatoes, and half a lobster coated with mayonnaise were brought to the table. Maigret refilled their glasses.

"After you called me, I told her that I would have to leave her for an hour or two, and she retorted, sourly:

" 'Naturally, your husband needs you. All men are the same. . . .'

"Then, abruptly changing the subject, she went on:

" 'When I am a widow, my pension won't even stretch to keeping this apartment, where I have lived for twenty-five years.' "

"Did she make any mention of there being another woman in Lognon's life?"

"Only obliquely. She remarked that police service was a degrading occupation, involving, as it did, hobnobbing with riffraff of every sort, prostitutes included."

"Did you try to find out whether she'd noticed any change in him of late?"

"I did, and her reply was:

" 'Ever since I was fool enough to marry him, he's told me periodically that he's on to something really big, which will at last bring him the recognition and promotion he deserves. . . . At first, I believed him and rejoiced with him. . . .

" 'But it was always the same; either the big case would fizzle out or someone else would get the credit!' "

Madame Maigret, looking more playful than Maigret could ever remember seeing her, added:

"I may as well tell you that, judging by the look she gave me as she said this, I was left in no doubt that you were the one she blamed for stealing all the credit. . . . As to recent events, her main complaint is that lately he's been burdened with more than his fair share of night duty. Is that true?"

"It was at his own request."

"He didn't admit that to her. . . . Apparently, for the past four or five days, he's been very self-important, saying that something big was about to happen, and that, this time, the papers would have no choice, whether they liked it or not, but to print his picture on the front page. . . ."

"Didn't she try to get any more out of him?"

"She didn't believe him, and I daresay she just sneered. Wait a minute, though! She did say something else that struck me as odd. She told me he had said:

" 'People aren't always what they seem, and if one could see behind the façade, one would find a good many things one wasn't expecting. . . .' "

They were interrupted at this point by the proprietor, who came to their table to pay his respects and offer them a liqueur on the house. When they were alone again, Madame Maigret asked, a little anxiously:

"Will you be able to make use of any of this, or have I been wasting your time?"

Because he was in the middle of lighting his pipe, he made no immediate reply. Besides, he was preoccupied with the germ of an idea beginning to take shape in his mind.

"Did you hear me?"

"Yes. I fancy that what you have just told me alters the whole complexion of the case. . . ."

She stared at him, torn between incredulity and delight. For the rest of her life, that lunch at Chez Manière was to remain one of her happiest memories.

3 / The Loves of Marinette

The rain was beginning to abate a little. It was no longer pelting down, beating upon the backs of the unwary. Maigret, gazing out the window, was in no hurry to break up this exceptionally heartwarming lunch-hour tête-à-tête.

If Lognon had been able to see them, it would merely have inflamed his bitterness.

"Here am I, lying on my bed of pain, while they take advantage of my plight to meet for lunch like young lovers at Chez Manière, and talk of my poor wife as an old bitch or a half-wit. . . ."

A thought struck Maigret, which he would not have claimed to be either original or profound:

"It's odd the way a man's susceptibilities can often cause more complications than his actual shortcomings or the lies he tells. . . ."

This was particularly true of his own profession. He could recall inquiries that had dragged on for days longer than necessary, sometimes even for weeks, because he dared not put a blunt question to a colleague, or because that colleague was inclined to shy away from certain topics.

"Are you going back to your office?"

"I'll be calling in at Avenue Junot first. What about you?"

"I think—don't you?—that if I leave her on her own, she'll accuse you of neglect, of letting her lie there unattended, while her husband, as a result of his devotion to duty, is dying."

It was true. Madame Lognon, who did not live up to her angelic name, Solange, was quite capable of complaining volubly to the reporters who would soon be thronging to her door, and heaven alone could tell what the newspapers would make of it.

"Still, you can't possibly spend all your days and nights with her until such time as he may recover. You'd better see if you can come to some arrangement with the old girl with the rosary."

"Her name is Mademoiselle Papin."

"I daresay that, for a small consideration, she could be persuaded to spend a few hours a day in the apartment. If worst comes to worst, you could always engage a nurse."

By the time they left the restaurant, only a few sparse drops of rain were falling. They parted in Place Constantin-Pecqueur. Slowly, Maigret walked back along Avenue Junot, and spotted Inspector Chinquier coming out of one house and ringing the bell next door.

This was another delicate job, often with disappointing results. One disturbed people in the peace of their own homes, people to whom the very word "police" was unsettling and harassing, to probe into their little private concerns.

"Would you mind telling me whether, last night . . ."

Everyone already knew that there had been an attempted murder in their own street. Doubtless they felt themselves to be under suspicion. Besides, it was not always pleasant to have to tell a perfect stranger what one had been up to the previous night.

In spite of all this, Maigret would have liked to be in Chinquier's shoes, because a closer acquaintance with the avenue and its inhabitants, a better understanding of their private lives, would at least have provided him with a context for the dramatic climax, and perhaps even a solution to the puzzle.

Unfortunately, it was a task that, as a chief superintendent, he could not permit himself to carry out in person, especially because he was already under censure for his propensity to wander off here, there, and everywhere, instead of staying in his office to supervise his subordinates.

Only one solitary policeman remained on duty outside Marinette's building. Traces of blood were still visible on the pavement. The reporters and cameramen had disappeared, but the occasional passer-by was still stopping to take a brief look.

"Anything new?"

"Nothing, Chief Superintendent. It's all been very quiet."

In the lodge, the Saugets were lingering over their lunch. The night porter of the Palace Hotel was still unshaven and still wearing his hideous dressing gown.

"Don't let me disturb you. I'm just going up to the fourth floor for a minute or two, but first there are a couple of things I'd like to ask you. . . . Did Mademoiselle Augier, by any chance, own a car?"

"She bought herself a motorbike a couple of years back, but, after she'd had it only a few months, she was run into by a car, and decided to get rid of it."

"Where did she usually go for her holidays?"

"Last summer she went to Spain, and she was so brown when she got back that I didn't recognize her at first."

"Did she go alone?"

"With a girl friend, or so she told me."

"Did any of her girl friends visit her here?"

"No. Apart from the fiancé I mentioned, and the inspector who took to dropping in recently, she was mostly by herself."

"What about Sundays?"

"She would often go away on Saturday evening—she had to work Saturday afternoons—and come back on Monday morning. Hairdressing salons are mostly closed on Monday mornings."

"I presume she didn't go very far?"

"All I know is that she went swimming. She often talked of the hours she had spent in the water. . . ."

He plodded up the four flights of stairs, spent a quarter of an hour or more opening drawers and cupboards, examining the dresses and underclothes and all the other small possessions that reveal the tastes and personality of their owner.

Although none of her things were in the top price bracket, every item had been chosen with care. He found a letter, posted in Grenoble, which he had missed earlier. The handwriting was that of a man, and the letter was lively and affectionate in tone. It was not until toward the end that the Chief Superintendent realized that the writer was Marinette's father.

"Your sister is pregnant again, and that engineer hus-
hand of hers is more cock-a-hoop than if he had built
the world's largest dam. As for your mother, she's still
coping with those forty-odd infants of hers, and comes
home to us at night smelling wholesomely of wet
babies. . . ."

He found a wedding photograph, presumably of her
sister's wedding, which was obviously some years old.
Flanking the bridal couple were their parents, looking
stiff and awkward as they always do in such photographs,
a young man and his wife with a little boy of about three,
and, lastly, a girl with expressive, sparkling eyes, who
could only have been Marinette.

He put the photograph in his pocket. A few minutes
later, he was in a taxi on his way to the Quai. He returned
to his office, which he had not left until one o'clock that
same morning, after many hours of persistent effort to
arrive at the exact circumstances of the holdup.

He barely had time to take off his coat before Janvier
was knocking at his door.

"I've seen the brother, Chief. I got him in his office on
Rue Le Peletier. He's quite a bigwig in the firm."

Maigret showed him the wedding photograph.

"Is this he?"

Unhesitatingly, Janvier pointed to the father of the
little boy.

"Had he heard about what happened last night?"

"No. The papers were only just out. At first he insisted
that there must be some mistake. His sister was not the
sort to take flight or go into hiding, he said.

" 'She's so outspoken that I've had to caution her about
it more than once, because some people don't like it. . . .' "

"Did you get the impression that he had something to hide?"

Maigret had sat down and was fidgeting with his pipes. Finally, he picked the one he wanted and filled it slowly.

"No. I was very favorably impressed. He told me all about his family, without reservation. His father teaches English at the lycée in Grenoble, and his mother is matron of a day nursery. There is another sister, living in Grenoble. She's married to an engineer, and he fathers a child on her every year. . . ."

"I know. . . ."

Maigret forbore to add that his source was a private letter found in a drawer.

"After passing her *baccalauréat*, Marinette decided to move to Paris. Her first job was as a stenographer in a lawyer's office, but she didn't care for office work, so she took a course in beauty care. Her dream, according to her brother, is to open a beauty salon of her own."

"What about the fiancé?"

"She really was engaged. The young man, whose name is Jean-Claude Ternel, is the son of a Paris industrialist. Marinette introduced him to her brother. She was intending to take him to Grenoble to meet her parents. . . ."

It is always discouraging, in a criminal case, to come across so many decent, ordinary people. One can't help wondering how and why they ever got themselves mixed up in it.

"Does the brother know that Jean-Claude used often to spend the night in her apartment?"

"He hadn't much to say about it, but he did give me to understand that, although, as her brother, he couldn't openly give his blessing, he was well enough up on present-day mores not to be too censorious."

"In other words, an ideal family!" groaned Maigret.

"I thought he had considerable charm."

The apartment on Avenue Junot, which must be a reflection of Marinette's personality, also had charm.

"Be that as it may, I want her found as soon as possible. Has her brother seen her recently?"

"Not this last week, but the week before. Whenever she wasn't away in the country, she spent her Sunday afternoons with her brother and sister-in-law. They live in Vanves, overlooking the park, which, as François Augier says, is very convenient for the children. . . ."

"Did she have anything special to tell them?"

"She mentioned in passing that she'd met the most extraordinary man, and that, quite soon, she might have an equally extraordinary story to tell. Her sister-in-law teased her about it."

"Was she referring to a new fiancé?"

Janvier looked quite crestfallen at having so little of interest to tell.

"She swore not, saying that once was enough."

"Why did she break off with Jean-Claude?"

"She woke up, finally, to the fact that he was a weakling, incapable of standing on his own feet, and, besides, she had come to realize that he wouldn't be all that sorry to get out of the engagement. He twice failed his *baccalauréat*. His father then sent him to stay with friends in England. The experiment didn't turn out too well. In the end, his father found him a job of sorts in the Paris office of his firm, but his performance proved far from satisfactory. . . ."

"Would you mind finding out the times of trains to Grenoble last night and early this morning?"

Nothing came of this. If Marinette had taken the early train, she could have been at her parents' home by now. But neither her father, whom he had finally managed to reach at the lycée, nor her mother had seen her.

Once again, he had had to tread warily, to spare these good people as much anxiety as he could.

"Oh, no! I'm sure nothing has happened to her. . . . Don't worry, Madame Augier. By sheer chance, your daughter just happened to be a witness to an attempted murder last night. . . . No! Not in her apartment. It happened outside, on Avenue Junot. . . . For some reason that is not yet clear to me, she decided to disappear for a short time. I thought she might have taken refuge with you. . . ."

Having replaced the receiver, the Chief Superintendent turned to Janvier.

"Phew! What else could I say to her? . . . Lapointe interviewed the girls at the beauty salon this morning, and none of them knows where Marinette used to spend her Sundays. . . . She went out into the rain with no luggage, not even a change of clothing. She must have known that she couldn't register at a hotel without arousing suspicion.

"So, either she must be staying with a girl friend in whom she has complete trust, or she's gone to some quiet little place that she knows well, a secluded retreat of some kind, some rural inn on the outskirts, perhaps. . . .

"She's passionately fond of swimming. . . . It's not very likely, on her salary, that she could afford a day by the sea every weekend. But there are lots of possible places on the river, any river nearby, the Seine, the Marne, or the Oise. . . .

"I suggest you go to see this Jean-Claude character, and try to find out from him where they used to go together. . . ."

Moers was waiting his turn in the next-door office. He had with him a small cardboard box, containing the bullets and the three spent cartridges.

"The ballistics expert agrees with us, Chief. The gun used was a .763, almost certainly a Mauser."

"What about fingerprints?"

"I wonder what you'll make of this. Inspector Lognon's prints were all over the living room, even on the knobs of the radio. . . ."

"None on the television set?"

"No. In the kitchen, his prints were on the handle of the refrigerator, and on a can containing ground coffee. He had also used the electric percolator. . . . Why are you smiling? Am I talking nonsense?"

"No. Go on."

"Lognon drank from the glass and the cup. As for the bottle of brandy, it is covered with his prints and those of the girl. . . ."

"What about the bedroom?"

"No trace of Lognon. Not a single hair of his on the pillow, only one of hers. Not a speck of mud or damp anywhere either, though I understand it was pouring when Lognon arrived at Avenue Junot."

Moers and his men could be trusted not to miss a thing.

"It looks as if he sat for a long while in the armchair facing one of the French windows. It was during that time, I daresay, that he turned on the radio. At some time or other, he opened the window. I found some splendid prints on the handle, and one of his cigarette stubs tossed out onto the balcony. I see you're still smiling. . . ."

"Only because what you say confirms an idea that I've been mulling over ever since my wife told me about her visit to Madame Lognon."

Surely everything pointed to the conclusion that old Grumpy, reduced by his wife to a state of abject servitude, had at last broken his chains, and found compensation in an amorous adventure for his dismal home life on Avenue Constantin-Pecqueur.

"My dear fellow, I'm smiling at the thought of all his colleagues buying the notion that Lognon was transformed overnight into some sort of Don Juan. Now I'd stake my life on it that there was nothing of the sort between those two. For his sake, I could almost wish there had been.

"He spent his nights in the front room, the living room, most of the time sitting facing the French windows, and the girl, Marinette, trusted him enough to go to bed, in spite of his presence next door. . . ."

"Did you find anything else?"

"Traces of sand in the girl's flat-heeled shoes, the ones she must have worn on her trips to the country. It's river sand. We have hundreds of different samples upstairs, but it will take hours of work and a good deal of luck to match it."

"Keep me informed. . . . Is there anyone else next door waiting to see me?"

"An inspector from the Eighteenth Arrondissement."

"Has he a little brown mustache?"

"Yes."

"It must be Chinquier. On your way out, send him in to me."

It was beginning to rain again, a fine rain, more like a Scotch mist, which softened the light. The clouds in the sky were almost motionless, though coalescing imperceptibly to form a canopy of unrelieved gray.

"Well, Chinquier?"

"I've left my men to complete the door-to-door questioning. It's a blessing there aren't more than forty houses on each side! Even so, that entails questioning two hundred people, at least."

"It's the houses opposite I'm most interested in."

"With your permission, Chief Superintendent, I'll come to that in a minute. I guessed what you had in mind. I began by questioning the tenants of the building that poor Lognon is known to have visited. There's only one apartment on the ground floor, occupied by an elderly couple, the Guèbres, who have been away for a month, visiting their married daughter in Mexico. . . ."

He drew from his pocket a notebook, several pages of which were covered with lists of names and diagrams. He, too, had to be handled with kid gloves, to avoid giving offense.

"There are two apartments to each of the other floors. On the first floor, there are Madame Faisant, a widow who is a saleswoman in a couture house, and a couple named Lanier, who have private means. They rushed to the window as soon as they heard the shots, and saw the car drive off, but, unfortunately, weren't able to read the license plate. . . ."

With eyes half closed, Maigret, occasionally puffing at his pipe, listened abstractedly to the inspector's painstaking report, which came across to him as a prolonged droning sound.

He pricked up his ears, however, when mention was made of one Maclet, who lived on the second floor of the neighboring building. According to Chinquier, he was a creaking old gentleman, who had shut himself up in his apartment once and for all, and whose only recreation was to sit at his window, watching the antics of the world outside with sardonic amusement.

"He's crippled with rheumatism, and just manages, with the aid of two sticks, to hobble about his filthy apartment, where no cleaning woman is permitted to set foot. He orders the food he needs each day by means of a note left under the doormat, and the concierge takes the food up and leaves it outside his door.

"He has no radio, and never reads a newspaper. The concierge claims that he's a rich man, for all that he lives like a pauper. He has a married daughter, who has tried more than once to get him committed to a mental hospital. . . ."

"Is he really mad?"

"Judge for yourself. I had the greatest possible difficulty in persuading him to open the door. It wasn't until I threatened to come back with a locksmith that he finally let me in. When, at last, he did so, he inspected me slowly, from head to foot, and then said with a sigh:

" 'You're rather young for this sort of job, aren't you?'

"I told him I was thirty-five, and he retorted, two or three times over:

" 'A boy! A mere boy! . . . What does anyone know at thirty-five? Understanding comes with experience. . . .' "

"Did you get anything of interest out of him?"

"He talked mostly about the Dutchman who lives opposite, in that house we saw from the balcony this morning, the little private house with the top floor glassed in like an artist's studio. . . .

"It seems that this house was built fifteen years ago, by a man named Norris Jonker, who still lives there. He is now sixty-four, and is married, it seems, to a fine-looking woman much younger than himself."

Once again, Maigret regretted not having been able to carry out this work himself. He would have enjoyed meeting the rheumatic old misanthrope, who lived the life of a hermit in the heart of Paris, in the heart of Montmartre, and who spent his time observing the comings and goings of the people across the way.

"Suddenly he was positively garrulous, and owing to his habit of jumping from one subject to another, and interspersing the narrative with his own comments, I'm afraid I may not be able to report verbatim everything he said. . . .

"Later, I went to see the Dutchman, and I think I ought to tell you about him first. He's a pleasant man, cultured and stylish. He's a member of an extremely rich and well-known family in Holland. His father owns a bank in Amsterdam, Jonker, Haag and Company. . . . He has never shown any interest in banking, and he spent much of his early life traveling the world.

"When he discovered that he was never so happy as in Paris, he built his present house on Avenue Junot, leaving his brother Hans to run the bank after his father's death. . . .

"Norris Jonker has been quite content to receive his share of the dividends, and invest it in pictures. . . ."

"Pictures?" repeated Maigret.

"Apparently he owns one of the finest collections in Paris. . . ."

"Just a second! Presumably you rang the doorbell. Who answered it?"

"A manservant with very fair hair and pink cheeks, youngish . . ."

"Did you say you were a police officer?"

"Yes. He didn't seem surprised. He showed me to a seat in the entrance hall. . . . I'm no expert on paintings, but even I had heard of some of the signatures I was able to read, such as Gauguin, Cézanne, and Renoir. A lot of naked women . . ."

"Were you kept waiting long?"

"About ten minutes. There are double doors leading from the hall into the drawing room. They were open, and I caught a glimpse of a young woman with black hair. She was still in her dressing gown, at three in the afternoon! I may have been mistaken, but I had the feeling that she'd come down specially to take a look at me. . . . A few minutes later, the manservant led me through the drawing room into a study lined with books from floor to ceiling. . . .

"Monsieur Jonker received me wearing flannel trousers, an open-necked silk shirt, and a black velvet jacket. He has pure-white hair, and a complexion almost as rosy as his manservant's. . . .

"There was a tray with a decanter and glasses on his desk.

" 'Please sit down and state your business,' he said, without a trace of an accent."

It was plain to see that Inspector Chinquier had been impressed equally by the luxuriously appointed house, the pictures, and their distinguished Dutch owner.

"I confess, I didn't know where to start. . . . I asked him whether he had heard the shots, and he replied that he hadn't, adding that his bedroom was at the back of the house, facing away from Avenue Junot, and that, anyway, the walls were so thick as to be almost sound-proof.

" 'I have a horror of noise,' he said, and proceeded to pour me a glass of a liqueur that was not familiar to me. It was very strong, and tasted faintly of orange. . . .

"I said: 'Still, you must be aware of what occurred last night just across the street from your house?'

" 'Carl told me about it when he brought me my break-fast. That was about ten. Carl is my manservant. He's the son of one of our tenant farmers. He said Avenue Junot was in turmoil because a policeman had been shot by a gang of thugs.' "

"How did he seem?" asked Maigret, fidgeting with his pipe.

"Cool and smiling, and surprisingly courteous for a man who had been intruded upon without warning."

" 'If you wish to speak to Carl, he is at your disposal, but his room also faces the garden, and he has assured me that he heard nothing either.'

" 'Are you married, Monsieur Jonker?'

" 'Yes, indeed. My wife was very upset to learn what had occurred only a few yards from our door.' "

At this point in his narrative, Chinquier began to show signs of uneasiness.

"I don't know whether I did the right thing, Chief Superintendent. I would have liked to ask him a lot more questions, but I hadn't the nerve, and I consoled myself with the thought that my first consideration should be to put you in the picture. . . ."

"Very well, then, let's get back to the old cripple."

"Yes. It's because of what he told me that I would have liked to discuss a number of things with the Dutchman. Almost the first thing Maclet said was:

" 'What would you do, Inspector, if you were married to one of the most beautiful women in Paris? . . . Ha! Ha! . . . You don't answer, I see. . . . And you are a long way short of your middle sixties! Let me put it another way. How would you expect a man of that age to behave, with a glorious creature like that always at his disposal? . . .

" 'Well now, the gentleman opposite must have rather peculiar views on this subject. . . . I sleep very little. I'm not much interested in current affairs, or in the various disasters of which the press and the radio make so much. . . .

" 'I spend my time thinking. . . . Do you see what I mean? . . . I look out the window and I think. . . . Few people seem to appreciate the entertainment value of thought. . . .

" 'Take the Dutchman and his wife, for instance. They seldom go out, once or twice a week at most, she wearing a long dress and he in a dinner jacket. They seldom get home later than one in the morning, which suggests that they enjoy nothing better than dining with friends or going to the theater. . . .

" 'They themselves never entertain in the evening. Nor do they give luncheon parties. . . . In fact, they seldom sit down to lunch before three in the afternoon.

" 'You see . . . one gets one's fun where one can. . . . One watches. . . . One makes guesses. . . . One endeavors to make sense of the scraps of information one has gathered. . . .

" 'Consequently, when one notices that, two or three times a week, a pretty girl rings the doorbell about eight in the evening, and doesn't leave the house until much later, often as late as the early hours of the following morning . . .' "

Maigret was decidedly sorry not to have been able to interview this eccentric old gentleman himself.

" 'But that's not all, Inspector. . . . Ah! my ramblings are beginning to interest you, I see. . . . You'll be even more interested when I tell you that it's a different young woman each time.

" 'They usually arrive in a taxi, but occasionally one comes on foot. . . . From my window, I watch them peering at the numbers of the houses. . . . And that, too, is significant, wouldn't you say?

" 'It means they have a prearranged appointment with someone at a specific address. . . .

" 'You see, I haven't always been an old sick animal gone to ground in his lair. There was a time when I knew quite a lot about women.

" 'Do you see that street lamp a few yards from their door? In the course of your work, you must have learned to recognize on sight the sort of woman who makes her living out of love, isn't that so? . . . And you must also be able to recognize the kind of girl who is on the fringes of the profession, night-club entertainers, for instance, or bit-part actresses in films or the theater, who are not above earning extra money that way, if the occasion arises. . . .' "

Maigret sprang to his feet.

"See here, Chinquier, do you get the point of all this?"

"What point?"

"How Lognon got involved in the first place. He often

spent the night on Avenue Junot, where he was on speaking terms with most of the people living there. . . . Let's suppose that he had several times spotted women such as you describe being admitted to the Dutchman's house. . . ."

"I thought of that, too. But there's no law against a man, even an elderly man, having a taste for variety."

And, indeed, it didn't offer an adequate explanation of why old Grumpy had sought and found a place from which to spy on that particular house, without being seen.

"I can think of another possibility."

"What?"

"That he was waiting for one of these late visitors to leave. He could have spotted one particular prostitute he'd had dealings with before. . . ."

"I see. . . . All the same, everyone is free to . . ."

"That depends on what was going on in the house, and what the girl had witnessed there. . . . What else did your nice old gentleman have to say?"

Maigret was becoming more and more intrigued by the queer old man at the window.

"I asked him every question that came into my head, and made a note of his replies."

Once more, Chinquier referred to his notebook.

"Question: 'Are you sure it wasn't the manservant that these women came to see?'

"Answer: 'For one thing, the manservant is in love with the girl in the dairy at the end of the street. She's a pudgy little thing, always ready to burst out laughing. She comes and waits for him outside, several nights a week. She stands in the shadows, ten yards or so away from the house—I could point out the exact spot—and it's never very long before he comes out to join her. . . .'

"Question: 'About what time would this be?' "

"Answer: 'Tennish . . . I presume he has to wait at table, and that his employers dine late. . . . The two of them go for a walk arm in arm, stopping occasionally to exchange a kiss, and, before parting, they retire into that little recess over there, and cling to one another for quite a long time. . . .'

"Question: 'Doesn't he see her home?'

"Answer: 'No. She skips off happily down the street by herself. . . . Sometimes she looks for all the world as if she's going to break into a dance. . . . And there's another reason why those women I told you about can't be there for the manservant. On several occasions, they've come while he was out.'

"Question: 'Who answered the door?'

"Answer: 'That's just it! How's this for an odd twist? Sometimes it's the Dutchman himself, and sometimes his wife. . . .'

"Question: 'Do they own a car?'

"Answer: 'Yes. One of those big American cars.'

"Question: 'Do they employ a chauffeur?'

"Answer: 'Carl does the driving, wearing a chauffeur's uniform.'

"Question: 'Are there any other living-in servants?'

"Answer: 'A cook and two housemaids . . . The maids never stay long.'

"Question: 'Do they have many visitors, apart from the ladies you mentioned?'

"Answer: 'A few . . . The most regular visitor is a man in his forties, an American, I would guess. He drives a yellow sports car, and generally calls in the afternoon.'

"Question: 'Does he stay long?'

"Answer: 'An hour or two.'

"Question: 'Doesn't he ever call in the evening or at night?'

"Answer: 'He did so twice, about a month ago, in company with a young woman. He was in and out in no time, leaving his companion behind in the house.'

"Question: 'Was it the same woman on both occasions?'

"Answer: 'No.' "

Maigret could picture the old man's smile, sardonic, perhaps even faintly salacious, as he watched these mysterious comings and goings.

"Answer: 'There is also another man, bald though quite young, who arrives at dusk in a taxi, and leaves carrying several parcels.'

"Question: 'What kind of parcels?'

"Answer: 'They could be pictures. . . . But then again they might be anything. . . . Well, Inspector, I think I've told you pretty well all I know. . . . It must be years since I last talked at such length, and I hope it may be years before I am called upon to do so again. . . . I'd better warn you, it would be a waste of time to summon me to a police station or a judge's chambers. . . .

" 'Still less can you depend on me to appear as a witness at the Assizes, if things should ever get that far. . . .

" 'We've had our little chat. . . . I've told you what I think. . . . Make whatever use of it you like, but I'm not going to allow myself to be put to further trouble on any pretext whatsoever.' "

Whereupon Chinquier proceeded to prove to Maigret that the local inspectors were well up to their job.

"After I had seen inside the Dutchman's house, I began to wonder whether the old man hadn't been leading me up the garden path. I thought to myself that if I could confirm one of his assertions, I could more readily believe the rest.

"After I left the old man, I called in at the dairy. I waited outside until the assistant was alone in the shop. She was exactly as he had described her, a plump country girl, looking as if she'd arrived so recently that she still hadn't got over her delighted astonishment at finding herself in Paris.

"I went in and asked her point-blank:

" 'Do you know anyone named Carl?'

"She blushed, looked uneasily toward an open door at the back, and murmured:

" 'Who are you? What business is it of yours?'

" 'I'm just making routine inquiries. I'm a police officer.'

" 'What have you got against him?'

" 'Nothing. It's a simple matter of checking a statement. Are you engaged?'

" 'We may get married someday, but he hasn't actually proposed to me yet. . . .'

" 'You see him several times a week, don't you?'

" 'Whenever I can . . .'

" 'I believe you wait for him a few yards away from the house on Avenue Junot?'

" 'Who told you?'

"At this point, an enormously fat woman suddenly emerged from the back room, and the girl had the presence of mind to raise her voice and say:

" 'No, sir. I'm afraid we're out of Gorgonzola, but we have Roquefort. . . . Roquefort and Gorgonzola taste very much alike. . . .' "

Maigret smiled.

"Did you have to buy some Roquefort?"

"I told her my wife wouldn't eat anything but Gorgonzola. . . . Well, that's the lot, Chief Superintendent. . . . I can't say, of course, what my colleagues may have to report tonight. . . . Any fresh news of poor Lognon?"

"I got someone to call the hospital a short while ago. The doctors still won't commit themselves, and he hasn't yet regained consciousness. They fear that the second bullet, which hit him below the shoulder, may have damaged the tip of his right lung, but he's in no fit condition to be X-rayed at present. . . ."

"I wonder what he could have found out to provoke an attempt at murder. . . . You'll be as baffled as I was when you meet the Dutchman. I just can't believe a man like that."

"There's just one more thing I'd like you to do, Chinquier. . . . When your men get back, and especially when the night-duty men come on, put them all to work finding out everything they can about the young women. Some of them, you tell me, arrived on foot on Avenue Junot, which suggests that they may live nearby. . . .

"Tell the men to go through all the night spots with a fine-tooth comb. . . . From your old gentleman's description, those girls don't sound the sort to walk the streets. Do you see what I'm getting at?"

"You think we may dig up one of the women who went to Avenue Junot. . . ."

No doubt, he would learn more from Marinette Augier, if he could find her. Would it be Moers and his lab assistants, with their samples of sand, who would finally put him on her track?

4/ A Visit to the Dutchman

"Netherlands Embassy, at your service."

The voice, which was young and fresh, with a slight accent, brought to mind windmills dominating a landscape, such as are sometimes depicted on cocoa cans.

"I would like to speak to the first secretary, please, mademoiselle."

"Who is this?"

"Chief Superintendent Maigret of the Department of Criminal Investigation."

"One moment. I'll just see if Monsieur Goudekamp is in his office."

After a brief pause, he heard the same voice again:

"Monsieur Goudekamp is in conference, but I'll connect you with the second secretary, Monsieur de Vries. . . . Hold on."

A man's voice, less fresh than the girl's, needless to say, and with a stronger accent.

"Hubert de Vries speaking, Second Secretary at the Netherlands Embassy."

"Chief Superintendent Maigret here, head of the Crime Squad."

"What can I do for you?"

Maigret could imagine Monsieur de Vries at the other end of the line, stiff and mistrustful. After all, he was only the second secretary as yet. No doubt he was fair, and a little too correctly dressed, as northerners so often are.

"I would like some information about a fellow countryman of yours who has been living in Paris for a long time, and whose name is probably familiar to you. . . ."

"Where are you speaking from, Monsieur Maigret?"

"From my office at the Quai des Orfèvres."

"I hope you won't take it amiss if I hang up and call you back."

Five minutes elapsed before the telephone rang.

"Forgive me, Monsieur Maigret, but we get called by all sorts of people, some of them assuming an identity other than their own. You wanted to talk to me about a citizen of the Netherlands living in Paris?"

"A Monsieur Norris Jonker . . ."

What was it that gave Maigret the impression that his invisible informant had suddenly been put on his guard?

"Yes . . ."

"Do you know him?"

"Jonker is a very common name in Holland, almost as common as Durand in France. And Norris is not an unusual Christian name."

"This particular Norris Jonker is related to the Amsterdam banking firm."

"The firm of Jonker, Haag and Company is one of the oldest in the country. Old Kees Jonker died some fifteen years ago and, if I am not mistaken, was succeeded by his son Hans."

"And Norris Jonker?"

"I don't know him personally."

"But you know of his existence?"

"Of course. I believe he's a member of the Saint-Cloud Golf Club. I may have seen him there without knowing who he was. . . ."

"Is he married?"

"To an Englishwoman, according to my information. Permit me to ask you a question, Monsieur Maigret. What is your interest in Monsieur Jonker?"

"He may have a very remote connection with a case I'm working on."

"Have you been to see him?"

"Not yet."

"Don't you think it would be simpler to put your questions to him directly? I could probably let you have his address."

"I have it."

"Norris Jonker hardly ever attends embassy functions. He is a member of a family that is not merely respectable but also highly distinguished, and I have every reason to believe that he himself is irreproachable. He is best known for his collection of paintings."

"What do you know of his wife?"

"I could answer more freely if I understood the drift of your questions. According to my information, Madame Jonker was born in the south of France, and subsequently married an Englishman, Herbert Muir, of Manchester, a manufacturer of ball bearings."

"Have they any children?"

"Not to my knowledge."

Maigret, realizing that this was not getting him any

further, brought the conversation to an end, and dialed another number, that of a licensed appraiser, who frequently appeared in the courts as an expert witness.

"Monsieur Manessi? Maigret here . . ."

"Hang on a minute, while I shut the door. . . . All right, continue. Dealing in pictures now, are you?"

"I don't know whether I am or not! Do you know a Dutchman by the name of Norris Jonker?"

"The one who lives on Avenue Junot? Not only do I know him, but I've been consulted by him regarding the authenticity of some of his purchases. He owns one of the finest collections of late-nineteenth- and early-twentieth-century paintings in existence. . . ."

"In other words, he's a very rich man?"

"His father was a banker and was himself a collector of paintings. Norris Jonker grew up surrounded by Van Goghs, Pissarros, Manets, and Renoirs. It's not surprising that he has no interest in banking. He inherited the greater part of his father's collection, and his income from the bank, which is now run by his brother, is sufficient to enable him to add to the collection."

"Do you know him personally?"

"Yes. Do you?"

"Not yet."

"He's more in the style of the English gentleman than a typical Dutchman. If I remember right, he got an Oxford degree, and stayed on in England for many years afterward. I've been told, in fact, that by the end of the last war he had attained the rank of colonel in the British Army."

"What about his wife?"

"She's a gorgeous creature. She was first married, very young, to an Englishman from Manchester."

"The manufacturer of ball bearings, yes, I know. . . ."

"I can't imagine why you should be taking so much interest in Jonker. I trust none of his pictures have been stolen?"

"No."

It was the Chief Superintendent, now, who was being evasive.

"Do they go out much?"

"Not as far as I know."

"Does Jonker move in artistic circles?"

"He attends the sales, of course, and is always in the know when anything good is coming up for auction at the Hôtel Drouot or Gallièra's or Sotheby's or in New York. . . ."

"Does he bid in person?"

"That's more than I can tell you. I know he used to travel a great deal, but whether he still does, I can't say. It's not necessary to be present to buy a picture at auction. Quite the contrary; it's becoming more and more common for the big buyers to bid through an agent. . . ."

"In other words, he's a man to be trusted?"

"With one's eyes shut."

"Thanks."

That didn't make things any easier. Reluctantly, Maigret got up and went to the closet to get his hat and coat.

The better known people are, the more important and highly regarded, the trickier it is to ring their doorbells and ask them questions. Such people are likely to complain to higher authority, which may result in unpleasant consequences for the police officer.

He considered asking one of his inspectors to accompany him, but in the end decided to go alone to Avenue Junot. He did not want his visit to look too official.

Half an hour later, he stepped out of a taxi at the door of the private house. Having presented his card, he was ushered into the hall by Carl, the white-jacketed manservant, just as Inspector Chinquier had been, but, perhaps owing to the Chief Superintendent's senior rank, he was kept waiting only five minutes, instead of ten.

"This way, if you please."

Carl led him across the drawing room, where, much to Maigret's disappointment, the beautiful Madame Jonker was not on view, and opened the study door. To all appearances, the Dutchman had not moved from his chair, or changed his clothes, since Chinquier's visit. He was seated at an Empire desk, studying engravings with the aid of an enormous magnifying glass fitted with a light.

He stood up at once, and Maigret was able to observe that he was exactly as he had been described to him. In his gray flannel trousers, his soft silk shirt and black velvet jacket, he was the very model of the casually dressed Englishman at home. He also had a good deal of English phlegm.

Showing no surprise or emotion, he inquired:

"Chief Superintendent Maigret?"

He waved his guest into a leather armchair on the other side of the desk, and sat down again.

"I am highly flattered, believe me, to receive a visit from a man as famous as yourself. . . ."

He spoke slowly, as if, even after so many years, he still thought in Dutch and had to translate every word.

"At the same time, I am a little surprised. This makes the second time I have been visited by the police. . . ."

He paused, staring down at his plump, well-kept hands.

Although he was by no means fat, he was what used to be called "a fine figure of a man," and in 1900 would have been much sought after as a model for drawings in *La Vie Parisienne*.

His face was a little flabby, and his blue eyes glinted behind rimless spectacles supported by thin, gold sidepieces.

Maigret, feeling not altogether at ease, began:

"Inspector Chinquier did, in fact, tell me that he had been to see you. He is a local man, and is connected only indirectly with my own branch of the force. . . ."

"Do you mean that you have come to check up on his report?"

"Not exactly. But it may be that he did not ask you as many questions as he might have."

The Dutchman, fidgeting with his magnifying glass, gave Maigret a straight look. There was more than a hint of mischief in his pale eyes, and also, perhaps, a touch of disingenuousness.

"See here, Chief Superintendent. I am sixty-four years of age, and I have seen a good deal of the world in my time. I settled in France many years ago, and built my house in Paris because I felt so much at home here.

"I have no police record, as they say here, and I've never so much as set foot in a police station or courtroom.

"I understand that last night shots were fired in the street, opposite my house. As I told the inspector, neither I nor my wife heard anything, because our bedrooms are on the other side of the house.

"Come now, tell me, how would you react if I were in your place and you in mine?"

"I shouldn't exactly welcome these visits. It is never very pleasant to have uninvited strangers charging into one's house."

"Come now, that's not what I'm complaining about. On the contrary, I welcome the opportunity of meeting someone of whom I have heard so much. My objection, as you must know, is on quite other grounds.

"Your inspector asked me a number of questions verging on the indiscreet. It might have been worse, I admit, given his occupation. I don't know what questions you intend to ask, but I confess it does surprise me that a man of your seniority should have thought fit to come in person."

"What if I were to tell you that it was out of respect for your position . . . ?"

"I should be flattered, but not necessarily convinced. Perhaps it would be wiser of me to ask what legal right you have to be here."

"I have no objection to that, Monsieur Jonker, and you are perfectly free to consult your lawyer. I may as well tell you that I have no warrant, and that you have every right to show me the door. On the other hand, you are no doubt aware that, should you refuse to co-operate, you would be taking the risk of being regarded as a hostile witness, if not as one who had something to hide."

The Dutchman, leaning back in his armchair, smiled, and stretched out his hand toward a box of cigars.

"You do smoke, I believe?"

"Only a pipe."

"Please yourself."

He himself chose a cigar, which he held against his ear and pinched, before snipping off the end with a good cigar cutter. Then very slowly, making something of a ritual of it, he lit it.

"One more question," he said, between two puffs of fine blue smoke. "Am I to understand that, of all the people living on Avenue Junot, I am the only one to be honored by a visit from you, or do you attach so much importance to this investigation that you propose to conduct all the house-to-house inquiries yourself?"

Maigret, in his turn, weighed his words with care.

"You are not the first person on the avenue whom I have thought fit to visit myself. As you surmise, house-to-house inquiries in general are being conducted by my inspectors, but in your case I felt I owed it to you to take the trouble. . . ."

The Dutchman nodded his thanks, but still looked unconvinced.

"In that case, I will do my best to answer your questions, but only insofar as they don't probe into my private life."

Maigret was opening his mouth to reply when the telephone rang.

"Excuse me."

Jonker picked up the receiver, and, frowning, proceeded to talk curtly in English to his caller. Maigret's schoolboy English was far from adequate. It had been of little use to him in London, and still less on the two occasions when he had visited the United States, although the people with whom he had come in contact there had been more than eager to follow his words.

All the same, he was able to gather that the Dutchman was saying that he could not talk freely, adding, in reply to a question from his invisible caller:

"From the same firm, yes . . . I'll call you back later."

What could he mean by this remark but that the inspector's earlier visit had been followed up by another from someone else in the same profession?

"Sorry about that . . . I'm all yours. . . ."

He settled himself more comfortably, leaning back a little in his chair and resting his elbows on the arms. Every now and again, he would examine the gradually lengthening white ash on his cigar.

"You asked me, Monsieur Jonker, what I would do if I were in your place. I can only reply to that by asking you to try to put yourself in mine. Whenever and wherever a crime is committed, there are always people in the neighborhood who, with prompting, are able to recall some odd little occurrence, the significance of which escaped them at the time."

"Tittle-tattle, do you mean?"

"Call it that, if you like. At any rate, we can't ignore such snippets of information. Admittedly, many turn out to be without foundation, but occasionally one such snippet may prove to be a vital clue."

"Can you give me an example?"

But the Chief Superintendent had no intention of blundering straight in. He was as yet unable to make up his mind whether the Dutchman was simply an honest man with a mischievous sense of humor, or a very shrewd and devious character, hiding his true self behind a show of candor.

"You are a married man, Monsieur Jonker?"

"Is that so surprising?"

"No. I am told that Madame Jonker is a very beautiful woman."

"I repeat, is that so surprising? Admittedly, I'm not

as young as I was; some might describe me as an old man, but they would have to add, in fairness, that I was well preserved.

"My wife is only thirty-four, which means that there is a difference of exactly thirty years in our ages. Do you imagine that ours is a unique case? I assure you that there are lots of couples like us, not only in Paris but everywhere. I see nothing especially remarkable in our situation."

"Is Madame Jonker a Frenchwoman by origin?"

"You are well informed, I see. Yes, she was born in Nice, but I first met her in London."

"I believe she has been married before?"

Jonker betrayed a hint of impatience, appropriate surely to any gentleman righteously shocked at such an intrusion into his private affairs, and particularly at the mention of his wife's name.

"She was a Mrs. Muir before she became Madame Jonker," he said, sounding more curt than hitherto.

He stared for some little time at his cigar, then added:

"I should tell you, moreover, since you have thought fit to raise the subject, that she didn't marry me for my money, since she was already, as they say, rich in her own right."

"For a man in your position, Monsieur Jonker, you very seldom go out."

"Is there anything wrong with that? Remember that the greater part of my life has been frittered away in going out and about, here, and in London, in the States, in India, in Australia, and a lot of other places besides. When you get to my age . . ."

"I'm not so very far off it. . . ."

"I repeat, when you get to my age, you will probably feel happier at home than at fashionable parties, or gambling clubs, or night clubs. . . ."

"Your attitude is the more understandable in that you must be very much in love with Madame Jonker. . . ."

This time, the former British Army colonel stiffened. He responded merely with a nod, which dislodged the ash of his cigar.

The awkward moment, which Maigret had postponed as long as he could, was approaching. He allowed himself a brief respite, in which to relight his pipe.

"You used the expression 'tittle-tattle,' and I am prepared to concede that some, at least, of our information falls into that category. . . ."

Was not the Dutchman's hand shaking a little? Be that as it might, he stretched it out for the cut-glass decanter and poured himself a drink.

"Would you care for a Curaçao?"

"No, thanks."

"Would you prefer whisky?"

Not waiting for a reply, he rang the bell. Almost without delay, Carl appeared.

"A bottle of Scotch, please . . . With soda or plain water?"

"Soda . . ."

During this brief interval both men were silent, and Maigret looked about him at the bookshelves, which covered the walls from floor to ceiling. Mostly, they were filled with art books, not only on painting but also on architecture and sculpture, from their earliest beginnings to the present day. Besides these books, there were bound volumes of all the important sales catalogues, going back forty years or so.

"Thanks, Carl . . . Have you told madame that I am busy?"

Out of politeness, he addressed the manservant in French.

"Is she still upstairs?"

"Yes, monsieur."

"And now, Chief Superintendent, I drink to your health, and await your account of the tittle-tattle you mentioned. . . ."

"I don't know whether the same is true of Holland, but Paris is full of people, mostly elderly people, who spend a good deal of their time looking out of their windows. . . . In this way, it has come to our notice that you frequently receive visitors at night. According to our information, two or three times a week sometimes, a young woman, always a different one, rings at your doorbell late at night, and is admitted to your house. . . ."

The Dutchman's ears had suddenly turned red. Instead of replying, he drew deeply on his cigar.

"I might have concluded that these visitors were friends of Madame Jonker but for the fact that they were all women of somewhat dubious reputation. It would have been insulting to your wife to infer that they could have been her friends. . . ."

He had seldom had to choose his words with such care. Indeed, he had seldom found himself in a more awkward position.

"Do you deny that these visits took place?"

"Since you have taken the trouble to come yourself, Chief Superintendent, I must assume that you are sure of your facts. Come now, don't prevaricate. Admit that if I were so foolish as to contradict you, you would confront me with one or more witnesses."

"You haven't answered my question."

"What exactly were you told about these young women?"

"I ask you a question and you fob me off with another."

"Well, I am in my own home, aren't I? If I were in your office, our respective positions would be different."

The Chief Superintendent thought it prudent to concede the point.

"Let us say, then, that the visitors in question could all be described as women of easy virtue. They don't merely go in and out, but spend the greater part, if not the whole, of the night in this house. . . ."

"That is so."

His glance did not waver. Quite the reverse, but his blue eyes had clouded over, so that they were now almost gray.

Maigret might not have found the courage to pursue the matter had he not thought of Lognon lying in the hospital, and of the unknown man who had viciously aimed a murderously powerful gun at his stomach.

Jonker gave him no help. His face was as impassive as a poker player's.

"If I am in error, please feel free to say so. I believed at first that the young ladies came to see your manservant, but then I learned that he had a steady girl friend, and that, on several occasions when the visitors in question called, he and she were out together.

"Would you mind telling me where exactly your manservant sleeps?"

"Upstairs, next door to the studio."

"Do the cook and housemaids also sleep on that floor?"

"No. The three women sleep in an annex built out into the garden."

"You often go to the door yourself, to admit your visitors at night. . . .

"Forgive me for mentioning that, according to my information, Madame Jonker, too, has been seen to open the door to them. . . ."

"It would appear that we have been under close surveillance. Our old village crones in Holland could scarcely do better. And now, perhaps, you would be so good as to tell me what possible connection there could be between the visits of these young women and the shots fired in the street?

"It is beyond belief to me that I personally should be a suspect, or that, for some reason as yet obscure, someone is attempting to involve me in this unsavory business. . . ."

"There's no question of that, and, to prove it, I will lay my cards on the table. The course of events last night, the type of weapon used, and other indications, which I am not at liberty to disclose, all lead me to the conclusion that the marksman is a professional criminal."

"Are you suggesting that I would have dealings with anyone of that sort?"

"Let me put a hypothetical case. You are known to be a very rich man, Monsieur Jonker. There are more works of art in this house than in many a provincial museum, no doubt of incalculable value. . . .

"Have you installed a burglar alarm in the house?"

"No. The real professional criminal, as you call him, can circumvent the most sophisticated of security equipment. If you want proof of this, you have only to refer to your own recent criminal records. I prefer to be well insured."

"Have you never been the victim of an attempted burglary?"

"Not to my knowledge."

"Are your servants trustworthy?"

"Carl and the cook, who have been with me for twenty years, most certainly are. I'm not so sure about the housemaids, but my wife never engages anyone without checking their personal references. You have still not explained the connection between what you call my lady visitors and . . ."

"I'm just coming to that."

So far, Maigret had managed to hold his own quite creditably. He rewarded himself with a gulp of whisky.

"Supposing a gang of art thieves, of which there are several scattered about the world, was planning to steal your pictures . . . Supposing a local inspector of police had got wind of the plan, but had insufficient evidence to enable him to take direct action . . . Supposing this inspector was watching this house from across the road last night, as he had done every night for the past few weeks, in the hope of catching the thieves in the act . . ."

"Surely, that would have been rather reckless of him?"

"In our job, Monsieur Jonker, we are sometimes obliged to take risks."

"Sorry."

"These gangs of art thieves, even though a killer may sometimes be found in their midst, are usually made up of clever, cultured people, who wouldn't dream of acting without the most careful preliminary investigation. . . . Since you tell me that you have every confidence in your servants, I can only suppose that one of these young women . . ."

Did Jonker accept the Chief Superintendent's reasoning at face value, or did he suspect a trap? It was impossible to tell.

"Many young women who work in night clubs and such are known to have contacts in what we in France call 'le Milieu,' in other words, the underworld."

"Are you asking me for the names, addresses, and telephone numbers of all the young women who have been to this house?"

His tone was not merely ironic now; it was acid.

"That might be a help, but what I would really like to know is what they come to your house to do."

Phew! This was the crunch. Jonker, motionless, his burned-out cigar between his fingers, was still looking him unblinkingly in the eye.

"Very well!" he said at last, rising to his feet.

And, having dropped his cigar stub in a blue ashtray, he took a step or two toward the middle of the room.

"I warned you at the outset of this interview that I was prepared to answer any question you might care to put to me, unless it was concerned with my private life. I admire you and congratulate you on the remarkable skill with which you have contrived to bring my private life into the discussion, by linking it with last night's unhappy events."

He stopped in front of Maigret, who was now also on his feet.

"I suppose you have been on the police force for a long time?"

"Twenty-eight years."

"I daresay your experience has not been wholly confined to the criminal classes. Is this really the first time you have encountered a man of my age and in my position who is a slave to his instincts? And do you regard it as entirely reprehensible?

"Paris can hardly be described as a puritan city, Chief Superintendent. In my own country, I would be pointed out in the street, perhaps even repudiated by my own family.

"There are many foreigners living here and on the Riviera who have chosen to make their home in France precisely because of the Frenchman's tolerant attitude in such matters. . . ."

"May I ask whether Madame Jonker . . . ?"

"Madame Jonker is a woman of the world, and no puritan. She knows that some men of my age need the stimulus of variety. . . . You leave me no choice but to speak of these extremely intimate matters. I trust you are satisfied. . . ."

He seemed to think that the interview was at an end, judging from the way he was looking toward the door.

But Maigret, speaking gently and in a very low voice, returned to the charge.

"Just now, you made some reference to names, addresses, and telephone numbers. . . ."

"You're not expecting me to provide a list, surely. People of that sort, though their lives may not be above suspicion, are not required to give an account of themselves to the police. It would be a gross impropriety on my part to place them in an equivocal position."

"You have admitted that you seldom go out, and that you are not in the habit of visiting night clubs. May I ask, therefore, how you make contact with your lady visitors?"

Another long pause for reflection.

"Do you really not know how these things are done?" he said at last, with a sigh.

"Needless to say, I am aware of the existence of pimps and procuresses, but their activities are illegal."

"Are their clients also in breach of the law?"

"At a pinch, a charge of complicity might be brought, but as a rule . . ."

"As a rule, their clients are not subject to harassment. Isn't that so? In which case, Chief Superintendent, I have no more to say to you."

"But I still have a favor to ask of you."

"Do you really mean a favor, or is that just a euphemism?"

The two men had now almost reached the point of open conflict.

"Heavens above! Well, if you must know, I might, if you were to refuse, be obliged to resort to the processes of the law."

"Well, what is it you want?"

"I would like to look over your house."

"Don't you mean search it?"

"You are forgetting that, up to now, I have proceeded on the assumption that you were an intended victim."

"And you are trying to protect me? Is that what you're saying?"

"Perhaps."

"Very well. Come with me."

Jonker was no longer the courteous host, offering drinks and cigars. His manner was suddenly very haughty indeed, quite that of the lord of the manor.

"You have already seen this room. I spend a good deal of my time in here. Do you wish me to open the drawers for you?"

"No."

"I should point out that there is an automatic in the

right-hand drawer, a Luger, which I acquired during the war."

He showed it to Maigret, adding:

"It's loaded. . . . I keep another gun, a Browning, in my bedroom. That, too, is loaded. I'll show it to you later. . . .

"This is the drawing room. I know you haven't come to admire my pictures. All the same, you might like to take a look at this Gauguin here. Many people consider it the artist's greatest work, and it will go to the museum in Amsterdam after my death. . . .

"Follow me. . . . Do you know anything about carpets? . . . There's nothing of interest to you here. . . . This is the dining room. The picture on the left of the mantelpiece is Cézanne's last painting. . . .

"This door here leads to a little room that my wife uses as her private sitting room. As you see, I have striven to create an atmosphere that is at once intimate and very feminine. . . .

"This is the pantry. . . . As you see, Carl is engaged in cleaning the silver. . . . It's seventeenth-century English silver. Its only drawback is that it is heavy to handle. . . .

"The kitchen is in the basement. . . . So is the cook. . . . Do you wish to see them?"

Whether intentionally or not, there was a touch of insolence in his easy manner.

"Very well, we'll go upstairs. . . . The staircase comes from an old château near Utrecht. . . . My own suite of rooms is on the left. . . ."

He opened doors in the manner of a real-estate agent conducting a prospective purchaser around a house.

"Another study, you see, like the one downstairs. I am fond of books, and find them very useful. . . . Those card indexes on the left-hand side record the individual histories of several thousand paintings, including a list of their successive owners, and the prices paid when any of them changed hands.

"Here is my bedroom. . . . The revolver I mentioned is in the drawer of the bedside table. . . . It's a common .635, not a very efficient offensive weapon. . . ."

Everywhere, even on the staircase, there were pictures, hung so close together as to be almost touching, and the best of them were to be found not in the drawing room but in the Dutchman's bedroom, a very dark room full of English furniture and deep leather armchairs.

"My bathroom . . . If you will give me a moment to make sure that my wife is not there, I'll show you her rooms across the passage. . . ."

He knocked, opened the door, and stepped inside.

"You may come in. . . . Her dressing room, with the two Fragonards that I chose specially for her. The armchairs once belonged to Madame Pompadour. If only you were here as an art lover instead of a policeman, Chief Superintendent, it would give me the greatest pleasure to linger over all our treasures with you. . . . My wife's bedroom . . ."

The walls were covered with crushed strawberry satin.

"Her bathroom . . ."

The Chief Superintendent did not go in, but he caught a glimpse of the bath, which was a sunken pool of black marble, with steps cut into the side.

"Let's go up to the top floor. . . . You have a right to see everything, isn't that so?"

He opened another door.

"Carl's bedroom . . . His bathroom is through that door

there. . . . As you see, he has his own television set. . . . He prefers black-and-white moving pictures to the works of the great masters. . . ."

He knocked on the door opposite, a heavy door richly carved, which had probably once adorned some château.

"May we come in, darling? I am showing Chief Superintendent Maigret over the house. He is the head of the Crime Squad. . . . That's right, isn't it, Chief Superintendent?"

Maigret received a shock. In the middle of the glass-walled studio, facing an easel, stood a figure all in white, which vividly recalled to his mind Lognon's word:

"Apparition . . ."

It was not an ordinary painter's smock that Madame Jonker was wearing. It was more like the habit worn by Dominican friars, and seemed to be made of some thick, soft material, such as Turkish toweling.

And, to cap it all, the Dutchman's wife's head was swathed in a white turban of the same material.

She had a palette in her left hand and a paintbrush in her right. Her black eyes were turned inquiringly on the Chief Superintendent.

"I have often heard about you, Monsieur Maigret, and I am delighted to meet you. Forgive me if I don't shake hands. . . ."

Having got rid of the paintbrush, she wiped her right hand on the white robe, leaving smears of green paint.

"I hope you're not a connoisseur of the arts. . . . But if you are, I beg you not to look at what I'm doing. . . ."

It was a shock to Maigret, after having seen so many masterpieces hanging on the walls downstairs, to find himself looking at a bare canvas spattered here and there with shapeless blobs of color.

5 / The Graffiti

At that instant something occurred that Maigret could not quite define, a change of tone, or, rather, a sort of shift of gears, as a result of which words, gestures, and attitudes took on a weightier significance. Was this due to the presence of the young woman, still draped in that peculiar garb, or had it something to do with the atmosphere of the room itself?

Logs were burning and crackling in the vast white stone fireplace, and the flames seemed to have an impish life of their own.

The Chief Superintendent now understood why the curtains, which could be seen from the windows of Marinette Augier's apartment, were almost always kept drawn. The studio was walled with glass on two sides, so that light could be let in from one side or the other, according to preference.

The curtains were of thick black hessian, now grayish from frequent washing, and they had shrunk, so that they no longer met in the middle.

The view on one side was of rooftops stretching as far as Saint-Ouen; on the other, with the sails of the

Moulin de la Galette in the foreground, almost the whole of Paris could be seen, including the layout of the boulevards, the large open space of the Champs-Elysées, the windings of the River Seine, and the gilded dome of the Invalides.

All Maigret's senses were alert, but it was not the view that fascinated him. It is difficult for anyone finding himself suddenly in an unfamiliar environment to grasp the whole of it, but Maigret felt that he was on the way to doing so.

Everything impinged on him at the same time, the two bare walls, for instance, painted a harsh white, with the vibrant flames of the fire flickering in the middle of one of them.

Madame Jonker had been working on a painting when the two men had come into the room. Did it not follow, therefore, that there should have been other paintings hanging on the walls? And also, as in any artist's studio, canvases stacked one against another on the floor? The expanse of polished boards, however, was as bare as the walls.

Next to the easel was a small table, on which stood a box full of tubes of paint.

Another table farther off, a table of white unvarnished wood, the only undistinguished object he had so far seen in that house, was covered with a jumble of pots, cans, bottles, and rags.

The only other furniture in the studio consisted of two antique wardrobes and two chairs, one upright, the other an armchair upholstered in fading brown velvet.

He could sense that something was amiss, though he could not say what. He was very alert, so that he was the more struck by the Dutchman's next words, addressed to his wife.

"The Chief Superintendent has come not to admire my pictures, but, strange as it may seem, to discuss the subject of jealousy. Apparently, he is surprised to learn that not all women are jealous. . . ."

It sounded a commonplace enough remark in spite of its ironic tone. But to Maigret's ears it was a clear warning from Jonker to his wife, and acknowledged by her with a flicker of the eyelids.

"Does your wife suffer from jealousy, Monsieur Maigret?"

"To tell you the honest truth, madame, she has never shown the slightest sign of it."

"Still, you must have interviewed a great many women at your office in your time."

He thought he had intercepted another signal, but this time addressed to him. Could he have been wrong?

The impression was so strong that he began to search his memory. Had he seen this woman before? Had she ever been up before him at headquarters? Their eyes met. Her beautiful face still wore the vague smile of a hostess receiving a guest. But was there not something more to be read in those great brown eyes, with their long, flickering lashes?

"Please don't interrupt your work on my account," he murmured.

For she was laying her palette down on the table. When she had done so, she unwound the white turban from her head and shook her black hair into its natural loose waves.

"I believe you are French by origin?"

"Norris told you, I suppose?"

It was a harmless enough question. Was he imagining things, or did it really suggest some other, hidden meaning?

"I already knew before I came here."

"So you've been making inquiries about us?"

Jonker was less relaxed than he had been in his study on the ground floor, or when, looking somewhat contemptuous, he had taken Maigret on a lightning tour of the house, explaining each room as if he were an official guide showing a visitor through an old château.

"You must be tired, darling; why not go and rest?"

Another signal? An order?

She took off the white burnoose that enveloped her, and emerged wearing a clinging black dress. At once, she seemed taller. She had the well-rounded figure of an attractive woman of mature years.

"When did you first take up painting, madame?"

Instead of replying directly, she explained.

"Living in a house full of pictures, and being married to a man whose only passion is art, one could hardly avoid the overwhelming temptation to try one's own hand with a paintbrush. I could scarcely attempt to compete with the great masters, whose works look down on me from morning to night, so I had to content myself with abstract painting. But please don't embarrass me by asking what this daub of mine is supposed to mean. . . ."

All the years she had spent in England and in Paris had not wholly wiped out her southern French accent, and Maigret noted every nuance of her speech with ever closer attention.

"Were you born in Nice?"

"So they told you that, too?"

It was his turn to look into her eyes and signal a message.

"I greatly admire the church of Sainte-Réparate. . . ."

She didn't blush, but almost imperceptibly flinched.

"I see you know the town."

By naming the church, he had evoked the whole of the old quarter of Nice, the poorest part of the town, with its narrow streets where the sun did not often penetrate, and where lines of washing were strung between the houses from one year's end to another.

He was now almost sure that she had been born in that district, in one of the crumbling tenements that each housed fifteen or twenty families, their staircases and back yards swarming with children.

It even seemed to him that she had implicitly admitted as much, and that, unknown to her husband, who was blind to these subtleties, he and she had exchanged what almost amounted to a masonic sign.

Chief superintendent and head of the Department of Criminal Investigation's Crime Squad Maigret might be, but he was still a man of the people.

As for her, live as she might among paintings worthy of the Louvre, buy her clothes as she might from the top couture houses, glitter as she might have done in diamonds, rubies, and emeralds at innumerable grand evening parties in Manchester and London, she had still grown up in the shadow of the church of Sainte-Réparate, and he would not have been surprised to learn that she had haunted the terraces of the Place Messéna with an armful of flowers to sell.

Both were now playing a role, as if beneath the words spoken between them flowed other words which were no concern of the son of the Dutch banker.

"Did your husband build this magnificent studio spe-cially for you?"

"Oh, no! . . . He hadn't even met me when he built the house. . . . He had a very dear friend who was a real artist. . . . She still exhibits at various art galleries. . . . I can't think why he didn't marry her. Maybe he wanted someone younger. . . . What do you say, Norris?"

"I don't remember. . . ."

"Well! How's that for good manners and delicacy?"

"I asked you just now when you started painting."

"I don't know. . . . A few months ago."

"I presume you spend part of each day up here in the studio?"

"This really is a grilling!" she said, banteringly. "Any-one could tell from the questions you ask that you are neither a woman nor a housewife. If you were to ask me, for instance, what I was doing at this time yesterday, I would probably find it difficult to answer. . . . I'm lazy, and it's my belief, contrary to what is usually said, that time passes more quickly for lazy people than for others.

"I get up late. . . . I dawdle. . . . I gossip with my maid. . . . The cook comes up to my room to get her orders. . . . It's lunchtime before I have really waked up to the fact that the day has begun."

"You're very chatty all of a sudden, my dear."

Maigret intervened:

"I didn't realize that it was possible to paint at night."

This time, it was impossible to miss the look that passed between husband and wife. The Dutchman forestalled whatever reply his wife had intended to make.

"It wouldn't have been, I daresay, for the Impression-ists, obsessed as they were with the interplay of sunlight and shade, but I know several modern painters who claim that artificial light brings out some colors better than daylight. . . ."

"Is that why you paint at night, madame?"

"I paint whenever I happen to feel the urge."

"And you usually feel the urge after dinner, and often work on at your easel until two in the morning. . . ."

She forced a smile.

"Well, really! I don't seem to be able to hide anything from you. . . ."

He pointed to the black curtains that covered the glass bay overlooking Avenue Junot.

"Look at those curtains over there. They no longer meet in the middle. In my experience, there is at least one insomniac to be found in every residential street. I mentioned this to your husband, when we were talking just now. The more educated among them read or listen to music. The others look out their windows. . . ."

Jonker had by now surrendered the initiative to his wife, as if he felt that he was out of his depth. He was nervous, but pretended to be listening to the conversation with only half an ear. Two or three times he went to the window, to gaze at the panorama of Paris spread out below.

The sky was growing lighter and lighter. It was white all over, and becoming more and more luminous, especially to the west, where it was almost possible to discern the sun dipping toward the horizon.

"Do you keep all your canvases in these cupboards?"

"No . . . Would you like to check? . . . I don't object to your prying. . . . After all, you're only doing your job. . . ."

She opened one of the wardrobes, which contained rolls of drawing paper, and more tubes of paint, bottles, and cans, all in a muddle, like those on the table.

The other wardrobe was empty, except for three blank canvases bearing the label of a supplier on Rue Lepic.

"You look disappointed. Were you hoping to find a skeleton?"

She was referring to the English saying to the effect that every family has a skeleton in its cupboard.

"Skeletons don't occur overnight," he said, frowning. "For the present, Lognon is still alive in his hospital bed. . . ."

"Lognon? That's an odd name. Who is he?"

"An inspector of police . . ."

"The one who was shot last night?"

"Are you quite sure, madame, that you were in your bedroom when the shot was fired, or I should say, the three shots?"

"I think, Chief Superintendent," interposed Jonker, "that this time you really are going too far. . . ."

"In that case, you may prefer to answer for her. Madame Jonker spends a good deal of her time painting, especially at night, often until very late. . . . And yet I find her in a virtually empty studio."

"Is there any French law that obliges a householder to fill his studio with furniture?"

"One would at least expect to find a great many paintings, some in progress, some completed. What do you do with your paintings, madame?"

Once again, she and her husband exchanged glances. Was she not, in effect, telling him to answer for her?

"Mirella doesn't claim to be a serious artist. . . ."

It was the first time Maigret had heard her referred to

by name. No doubt she had originally been called Mireille.

"Most of her paintings she destroys after she's finished them. . . ."

"One moment, Monsieur Jonker . . . I'm sorry to have to be so persistent. I've met one or two painters in my time. . . . How would they set about destroying a painting?"

"They'd cut it into strips and burn it, or put it in the trash can. . . ."

"I mean before that?"

"I don't understand you."

"And you such an expert? You surprise me. Are you suggesting that they throw away the stretchers as well? Look, there are three stretchers in this cupboard, all brand new. . . ."

"If my wife isn't too dissatisfied with a picture, she will sometimes give it to a friend. . . ."

"Are you referring to the paintings that are collected from her at night?"

"At night, or during the day . . ."

"If those are your wife's work, then she's more prolific than she has led me to believe. . . ."

"They're not all hers. . . ."

"Is there anything else you need me for?" inquired Madame Jonker. "Why don't we all go downstairs and have a cup of tea?"

"Not just now, madame. Your husband has been kind enough to show me over the house, but I have not yet seen what is behind this door, here. . . ."

It was a massive door of blackened oak, at the far end of the studio.

"Who knows? We might even find one or two of your elusive paintings in there."

The tension in the air was like a charge of electricity. The voices, though more muted, sounded sharper.

"I'm afraid not, Chief Superintendent."

"How can you be so sure?"

"Because that door hasn't been opened for months, if not for years. . . . It belonged formerly to the person my wife spoke of. . . . She used to go in there to rest between sessions at her easel. . . ."

"And you have kept it as a shrine for all these years?"

He was deliberately pressing home the attack, in the hope of provoking an unguarded response from his adversary. The time had come, he felt, to exploit his advantage to the limit, and this time, by exception, the climax had been reached, not in his office on the Quai des Orfèvres, but in an artist's studio, from which could be seen a panoramic view of Paris.

The Dutchman's fists were clenched, but he still did not lose his self-control.

"I am quite sure, Chief Superintendent, that if I were to burst unexpectedly into your home, and root in corners and harry your wife with question after question, I would discover a great many things that would strike me as peculiar, if not inexplicable. Surely you must realize that everyone has his own personal habits, his own special ways of looking at things, which are incomprehensible to any outsider. . . .

"This is a fairly big house. . . . Practically all my time is taken up with my pictures. . . . Our social life is severely restricted, and my wife, as she has told you, likes to amuse herself with a paintbrush. Is it so very surprising that she should attach little importance to what becomes of her paintings, whether they are burned, thrown in the trash can, or given away to friends?"

"What friends?"

"You leave me no choice but to repeat what I said earlier in my study. It would be most improper of me to forget myself so far as to involve a third party in the sort of unpleasantness my wife and I are now having to put up with because shots were fired in our street by persons unknown. . . ."

"To get back to the question of this door . . ."

"I don't know how many rooms you have in your apartment, Chief Superintendent, but there are thirty-two in this house. There are four servants always coming and going. We have occasionally had to dismiss one of the maids for improper conduct. . . .

"Given these conditions, it is surely not surprising that a key should occasionally get lost?"

"And you haven't had a new one made?"

"It never occurred to me."

"Are you sure the key is not in the house?"

"Not as far as I know. If it is, I daresay it will turn up one day in the most unlikely place. . . ."

"Do you mind if I make a phone call from here?"

There was an extension telephone on the table. Maigret had noticed that there was one in almost every room in the house. No doubt they could be used for both internal and external calls.

"What do you intend to do?"

"Send for a locksmith . . ."

"I don't think I can allow that. It seems to me you're exceeding your authority. . . ."

"Very well, I'll call the Department of Public Prosecutions, which will issue a warrant, duly signed, and deliver it to me here. . . ."

Once more, husband and wife exchanged glances. It was Mirella who made the first move. She went across to a wardrobe, carrying the stool that had been standing in front of the easel. She climbed onto it, stretched out her arm, and ran her hand along the top. When she lowered her arm, she was holding a key.

"You see, Monsieur Jonker, there was something that struck me as odd, or, rather, two related things. There is a bolt on the door of this studio, but, contrary to the usual practice, it is fixed to the outside of the door.

"Just now, while you were talking to me, I noticed that the same is true of this other door. . . ."

"You're perfectly entitled to express surprise, Chief Superintendent. Indeed, you have done little else since you came into this house. Your way of life is so very different from ours that you couldn't be expected to understand."

"I'm doing my best, as you can see. . . ."

He took the key that Madame Jonker held out to him and went across to the locked door. While his two companions stood motionless, as if rooted to the floor in the middle of the vast studio, he tried the key in the lock.

"How long did you say it was since this door was last opened?"

"What does it matter?"

"I won't ask you to join me here, madame, and I'm sure you can guess why, but I should be obliged if your husband would do so. . . ."

The Dutchman came forward, determined to keep his end up.

"To begin with, please note that this floor is clean. There isn't a speck of dust anywhere, and, if you touch it, you will see that it is damp in places, as if it had been scrubbed down very recently. . . . In fact, the room was cleaned last night or this morning. Who did it?"

It was Mirella who spoke, her voice coming from behind him.

"It certainly wasn't me. . . . You'd better ask the maids . . . unless my husband gave instructions to Carl. . . ."

It was quite a small room. The window, like the glass bay in the studio, looked out on the panoramic view of Paris, and the shabby flowered curtains were spattered with paint. It looked, in fact, as if someone, after having been painting with his fingers, had wiped his hands on them here and there.

There was an iron bedstead in one corner, with a mattress on it, but no sheets, no blankets.

The most striking aspect of the room was what Maigret could only call "graffiti." On the dirty white walls, some-one had amused himself by delineating obscene figures in outline, such as one sometimes sees in public lavatories. The only difference was that these were not pencil drawings, but were done with oil paints in green, blue, yellow, and violet.

"I will not make so bold, Monsieur Jonker, as to ask you whether you think these murals were done by your former friend. Indeed, this sketch here rules out any such supposition. . . ."

It was a portrait of Mirella, executed by means of a few bold strokes, and it was a good deal livelier than many of the paintings hanging in the drawing room.

"You are waiting for an explanation, no doubt?"

"Does that surprise you? As you said yourself, your

life style and mine are very different. Perhaps I do find it a little difficult to understand your behavior. Be that as it may, I am none the less convinced that your own friends, members of your own social class, would be very much surprised if they were to discover these—er—let's call them frescoes, under your roof. . . ."

Not only had someone portrayed, with a wealth of detail, those parts of the human body normally kept covered, but there were also scenes of unbridled eroticism. In contrast, the wall near the bed was covered with vertical lines, which reminded the Chief Superintendent of those drawn on prison walls to mark the passage of time.

"Why did the person who lived here count the days so impatiently?"

"What do you mean?"

"Didn't you know of the existence of these graffiti?"

"I did take a look around in here some time ago."

"How long ago?"

"Several months, as I told you. . . . I was shocked by what I saw, so I double-locked the door and put the key on top of the wardrobe. . . ."

"In the presence of your wife?"

"I don't remember."

"You have seen these murals, have you not, madame?" She nodded.

"What were you feelings when you saw the portrait of yourself?"

"I don't call that a portrait. It's just a rough sketch, a doodle such as any painter might draw. . . ."

"I'm waiting for one or both of you to tell me what this is all about."

There was a long silence, during which Maigret, without waiting for permission, took his pipe out of his pocket.

"I wonder whether it wouldn't be best," murmured the Dutchman, "for me to call in my lawyer. I am not sufficiently familiar with French law to know whether or not you have the right to interrogate us like this."

"If you choose to call in your legal adviser now, rather than to give me a straight answer, I suggest you arrange for him to meet you at the Quai des Orfèvres, because, if that is your decision, I must ask you to accompany me there at once."

"Without a warrant?"

"With or without a warrant. If necessary, I can have a warrant delivered here within half an hour."

The Chief Superintendent went toward the telephone.

"Wait!"

"Who occupied that room?"

"It's an old story. . . . Why don't we go downstairs and have a drink while we talk? I could do with a cigar myself, and I haven't got one on me. . . ."

"On condition that Madame Jonker comes with us."

She went first, looking weary and perhaps resigned. Maigret followed, with Jonker close on his heels.

"In here?" asked Mirella, when they reached the drawing room.

"I'd rather we went into my study. . . .

"What can I offer you, Monsieur Maigret?"

"Nothing for the moment . . ."

She looked toward the glass from which he had drunk earlier, standing next to her husband's on the desk. Was it because the situation had changed that the Chief Superintendent had this time refused a drink?

The room was darker now. The Dutchman switched on the lights and poured himself a glass of Curaçao. He looked inquiringly at his wife.

"No. I'd rather have whisky. . . ."

He was the first to decide to sit down, assuming almost the identical posture in which he had sat an hour earlier. His wife remained standing, with a glass in her hand.

"Two or three years ago," began the art lover, snipping the end of his cigar.

The Chief Superintendent interrupted him.

"I wish you would be more precise. Ever since I got here, you have not mentioned a single date or name, unless we are to include the names of painters long since dead. . . . You talk in terms of several weeks, several months, or several years. . . . Instead of stating the time, you say early evening or late at night."

"Maybe it's because I don't take much account of time. Remember, I have no office to go to or leave at any particular time, and, until today, I have never been called upon to give an account of myself to anybody."

He was overdoing the aggressive arrogance. It didn't ring true any more. Maigret caught a look of mingled anxiety and disapproval on his wife's face.

You, my dear, he thought, know from experience that that particular line cuts no ice with the police. . . .

Was it in Nice, when she was a mere girl, or in England that he had had dealings with her?

"It's up to you whether you believe me or not, Chief Superintendent. . . . I repeat that, two or three years ago, I was told of a talented young painter who was so down on his luck that he sometimes had to sleep under the bridges and forage for food in trash cans. . . ."

"You say you were 'told' of this young man. Who by? A friend, an art dealer?"

Jonker made as if to brush away a fly.

"What does it matter? I don't remember. At any rate, I felt a twinge of guilt when I thought of that studio up there going to waste. . . ."

"This was before your wife took up painting, then?"

"Yes . . . I wouldn't have had him here . . ."

"What is the name of this graffiti merchant?"

"I never knew his surname."

"What was his first name?"

A slight pause:

"Pedro."

It was plain to see that this was pure invention.

"A Spaniard? An Italian?"

"Believe it or not, I never bothered to ask. I put the studio and adjoining bedroom at his disposal, and gave him enough money to buy paints and canvas."

"And at night you locked him in to prevent him from going out on the town?"

"I didn't lock him in."

"What, then, was the point of the bolts on the outside of the doors?"

"They were put there when the house was built."

"What for?"

"For a very simple reason. As you are not a collector, it would probably not occur to you. For a long time, I used the studio as a storeroom for such paintings as I had no room to display on my walls. It's quite natural that I should bolt the door from the outside, since I could hardly do so from inside."

"I thought you said that the studio had been built for the use of your former artist friend. . . ."

"Let's say the bolts were put on after she had ceased to live here. . . ."

"Including the bolt on the bedroom door?"

"I'm not even sure that it was on my instructions that it was put there. . . ."

"To return to Pedro . . ."

"He lived in the house for several months. . . ."

"*Several!*" exclaimed Maigret, stressing the word. Mirella could not help smiling.

The Dutchman was growing restive. He must have exercised a great deal of self-control to keep his temper.

"Was he genuinely talented?"

"Very much so."

"Did he make a success of his career? Did he achieve recognition?"

"I don't know. . . . I occasionally used to go up to the studio, and I admired his work."

"Did you buy any of his pictures?"

"How could I buy pictures from a man who was dependent on me for bed and board?"

"So you don't possess a single one of his works? . . . Did it not occur to him to make you a present of one or two before he left?"

"Have you seen a single painting in this house that is less than thirty years old? . . . A love of paintings often turns a man into a collector. . . . And collectors as a whole prefer to specialize in one particular field. My own special field begins with Van Gogh and ends with Modigliani."

"Did Pedro have all his meals upstairs?"

"I suppose so."

"Did Carl take them up to him?"

"I leave all that sort of thing to my wife."

"Yes, it was Carl," she said, without conviction.

"Did he go out much?"

"No more than any other young man of his age."

"How old was he, by the way?"

"Twenty-two or twenty-three. By the end of his stay he had made a good many friends, young men and women of his own age. At first, he never entertained more than one or two at a time.

"Then he began overdoing it. Some nights, there would be as many as twenty of them up there, making a fearful racket just above my wife's bedroom, preventing her from getting to sleep. . . ."

"Did it never occur to you, madame, to go upstairs yourself and find out what was going on?"

"I left that to my husband."

"And what was the outcome?"

"He threw Pedro out, but not, mind you, before he had given him some money."

"And it was then that you discovered the graffiti?"

Jonker nodded.

"And you, too, madame? If so, you must have realized, when you saw that portrait of yourself, that Pedro was in love with you. Did he ever make a pass at you?"

"You'd better not take that tone with my wife, Chief Superintendent; otherwise I'll be regretfully compelled to make a formal complaint to my ambassador," said Jonker, sternly.

"You won't forget to tell him, will you, about the young women who used to slink into the house after dark and stay the whole night?"

"I thought I understood the French character. . . ."

"I thought I understood the Dutch character. . . ."

Mirella intervened.

"Would you two kindly stop bickering? I can understand that my husband would be irritated by some of your questions, especially those concerning me. But I also understand that it is hard for the Chief Superintendent to approve of the sort of life we lead. . . .

"As far as those women are concerned, Monsieur Maigret, I've always known about them, even before we were married. You'd be surprised to learn how many husbands there are who share his tastes. . . . Most of them keep it dark, especially if they move among high-minded people. My husband prefers to be open about it, and I take that as a tribute to my intelligence and my affection for him. . . ."

He noticed that she didn't say "love."

"If some of his answers seem imprecise and apparently self-contradictory, I believe it is because he has nothing to hide. . . ."

"Very well, then, let me now put a question to you that requires a precise answer. Until what time, exactly, did you remain in your studio last night?"

"Let me think. I don't bother with wearing a watch when I'm working, and you yourself will have noticed that there are no clocks up there. . . . It was about eleven when I told my personal maid that she could go to bed. . . ."

"At that time, were you still up there?"

"Yes. She came in to ask me if I would be needing her help in getting ready for bed. . . ."

"Were you working on the painting that is still on the easel?"

"I spent a long time with a stick of charcoal in one hand and a rag in the other, trying to think of a subject."

"What is the subject of the painting?"

"Let's call it Harmony. . . . Abstract paintings are not mere daubs. . . . Possibly, they require more thought and entail more false starts than figurative paintings. . . ."

"Let's get back to the time. . . ."

"It could have been as late as one in the morning when I went downstairs to my room."

"Did you switch off the light in the studio?"

"I think so. It's the sort of thing one does automatically."

"Were you wearing the same white robe and turban as you were today?"

"To tell you the truth, it's only an old bathrobe and a Turkish towel. Since I paint only for recreation, it would have been pretentious of me to buy a real painter's smock."

"Had your husband gone to bed? Didn't you go in and say good night to him?"

"I never do if he goes to bed before me."

"Because you're afraid one of his lady visitors might be with him?"

"If you say so."

"I think we've almost reached the end. . . ."

He could feel a relaxation of tension, but he was only up to one of his favorite tricks. Slowly, he relit his pipe, apparently searching his memory for anything he might have overlooked.

"Earlier this evening, Monsieur Jonker, you made a point, as tactfully as you were able, of the fact that I lacked experience of the thought processes, actions, and behavior of an art connoisseur. I see from your library shelves that you keep abreast of all the important sales. You obviously buy lavishly, since there are times when you have to store some of your pictures in the studio because you have no room to hang them. . . .

"Am I to deduce from this that you sometimes sell pictures when you have grown tired of them?"

"For the last time, let me try to explain. I inherited a number of paintings from my father, who was not only a financial genius, but also one of the first men to discover those artists whose works are now sought after by every museum in the world.

"My income, large though it is, is insufficient to enable me to buy every picture I covet ad infinitum.

"As all collectors do, I started with the second-rate, or perhaps I should say with the minor works of the great painters. . . .

"Little by little, as these paintings appreciated in value and I became more selective in my tastes, I began to sell some of those lesser works, and replace them with better ones. . . ."

"Forgive me for interrupting. Have you continued this practice up to the present day?"

"And shall do, till I die."

"These paintings you sell, do you put them up for auction at the Hôtel Drouot, or do you entrust them to an art dealer?"

"I do occasionally, but not often, sell a picture at public auction. But most of the items that come up for auction form part of estates that are being settled. A collector prefers to go about things in a different way. . . ."

"How do you mean?"

"He studies the market. He knows, for instance, that such and such a museum in the United States or South America is on the lookout for a Renoir, say, or a blue-period Picasso. If he has such a painting to dispose of, he sets about making the right contacts. . . ."

"Which would explain how some of your neighbors happened to see pictures being taken away from your house?"

"Those, and my wife's paintings . . ."

"I wonder, Monsieur Jonker, if you would be willing to let me have the names of some of the buyers. Let's confine ourselves, say, to the past twelve months. . . ."

"No."

It was a cold and emphatic "no."

"Am I then to understand that these were clandestine transactions?"

"I don't care for the word 'clandestine.' Such transactions are always conducted discreetly. Most countries, for instance, have laws regulating the export of works of art, with a view to protecting their national treasures.

"It's not only that the museums have pre-emptive rights, but that export permits are not readily granted.

"There is, in the drawing room next door, one of Chirico's most important works, which was illegally smuggled across the Italian frontier, not to mention a Manet that, incredible as it may seem, came to me from Russia.

"Surely you must see that I can't possibly name names? Someone buys a picture from me. I hand it over to him, and he pays me. It's no concern of mine what becomes of it after that. . . ."

"You don't know?"

"I don't want to know. It's none of my business, any more than it is to find out where one of my own purchases comes from. . . ."

Maigret stood up. He felt as if he had been in this house for an eternity, and the luxurious trappings, so remote from real life, were beginning to oppress him. Besides, he was thirsty and, as things now stood between Jonker and himself, he was precluded from accepting a drink from him.

"Please forgive me, madame, for having disturbed you at your work, and ruined your afternoon. . . ."

Was there not an unspoken question in Mirella's eyes?

Surely this is not the end? they seemed to say. I know how the police go about their business. You don't intend to let us alone, and I'm wondering what trap you have in store for us. . . .

Turning to her husband, she seemed about to speak, hesitated, then murmured lamely to Maigret:

"It's been a pleasure to meet you. . . ."

Jonker, standing up, put out his cigar, and said in his turn:

"I'm sorry if I seemed short-tempered at times. One should not forget one's duty as a host. . . ."

The manservant was not summoned to see him out. The Dutchman himself preceded him to the door, and opened it. Outside, it was cool, and the air was damp and acrid with dust. Halos were beginning to form around the street lamps.

In the building opposite, Marinette Augier's windows were dark. So were the windows on the second floor of the house next door, but there was a face pressed against one of the windowpanes, the face of an old man.

Maigret was tempted to give a friendly wave to old Maclet, still faithfully at his post. He even felt inclined to go across and knock on his door, but he had more urgent matters to attend to.

These, however, did not prevent him from returning to the bistro he had patronized that morning and gulping down two large glasses of beer before getting into a taxi at the corner of Rue Caulaincourt.

⑥/ The Barefoot Drunkard

Habits are formed rapidly in local bistros. Because Maigret had had a hot toddy that morning, the proprietor, wearing his sleeves rolled up, seemed surprised that he now ordered beer. And when Maigret asked for a *jeton* for the telephone, he said:

"Only one?"

The man who had used the telephone before Maigret must have drunk a great deal of Calvados, because not only the telephone booth but the instrument as well reeked of fermented apples.

"Hello! Who is that speaking?"

"Inspector Neveu."

"Isn't Lucas there?"

"I'll get him. . . . One moment . . . He's speaking on another line. . . ."

The Chief Superintendent waited patiently, looking absently about him at the reassuring furnishings of the little café, the zinc counter, the bottles, with their familiar shapes and labels. The newspapers were much given to expressing complacency or anxiety about the dizzying speed of change in the modern world, yet here displayed

before his very eyes, after so many years, including those
of the Second World War, were brands of apéritif he used
to see on the shelves of the village inn when he was a
child.

"Sorry, Chief . . ."

"There's a man by the name of Norris Jonker, who
lives on Avenue Junot. I want the house put under surveillance as soon as possible. It's opposite the building
Lognon was leaving when he was shot. You'd better send
at least two men, with a car. . . ."

"I'm not sure there are any left in the forecourt. . . .
I'm afraid not. . . ."

"You'll manage somehow. . . . Not only do I want
Monsieur and Madame Jonker followed if they go out,
but I want a tail put on anyone who calls at the house.
. . . Be as quick as you can. . . ."

In the taxi, as it wound its way through the lighted
streets, Maigret was in a strange mood. He ought to have
felt pleased that he had not allowed himself to be overawed by the Dutchman, with all his pride and wealth, or
by the mature beauty of Mirella.

Seldom had he gathered so much information in a single day about a case of which he had known nothing
when he had got up that morning. Not only had he shaken
a great many little secrets out of the art collector and
his wife, but also he had learned much that he would
never have suspected about Avenue Junot itself.

Why, then, was he still not satisfied, but, rather, prey
to an indefinable anxiety? He forced these questions upon
himself, but it was not until they were crossing the Pont-
au-Change and were in sight of the old Palais de Justice,
so familiar to him, that he thought he had found the
cause of his uneasiness.

Although he had spent more time in Norris Jonker's study than anywhere else, and had been shown over the house from bottom to top, and although the drama had reached its climax in the studio at the top of the house, it was not any of these rooms that had made the greatest impression on him.

The scene that had etched itself on his memory, like the chorus of a song, was the little bedroom, with its iron bedstead, and he suddenly understood why he had felt uneasy.

He saw again, but magnified, as on a movie screen, the obscene pictures daubed on the white walls with thick brush strokes in green, yellow, and blue. When he tried to conjure up a picture of Mirella Jonker, it was her portrait, rapidly sketched with a few bold strokes, that came most vividly to his mind.

The man or woman who had made that sketch in a transport of passion, and surrounded it with so many nightmarish sexual symbols, must surely have been mad. He had seen paintings by certified lunatics that had had the same powerfully mesmeric and evocative effect on him.

The room had been recently occupied, there was no doubt about that. Otherwise, why should it have been thought necessary to scrub it down so thoroughly within the last few hours? And why had they not, at the same time, ventured to slap a fresh coat of whitewash on the walls?

Slowly, he went up the great staircase at police headquarters. Often he would not go straight to his office, but look in on the inspectors in their duty room. He did so now. Each sat working at his desk under the lighted ceiling globes, like a class of students at night school.

He was not looking for anyone in particular. It was just that he found it reassuring to resume contact in this way with his working surroundings.

Just as schoolchildren do not look up when the teacher passes by, neither did they; and yet there was not one who did not know that he was looking grave and anxious, and that his face showed signs not merely of weariness but also of exhaustion.

"Has my wife telephoned?"

"No, Chief."

"Try to get her at my home number. If she's not there, try Lognon's apartment."

Perhaps not a certified lunatic, confined in a psychiatric hospital, but certainly a violent man, with little or no self-control . . .

"Hello! Is that you?"

She was back in their apartment, and was no doubt making preparations for dinner.

"Have you been back long?"

"Over an hour. Actually, I don't think she was all that keen for me to stay. . . . She was flattered that I had put myself out for her, but she doesn't feel comfortable with me. She is much more at home with the old girl with the rosary. Alone together, they can have a good moan, and spend endless time totting up all their little misfortunes. . . .

"I went out to the shops again, and bought her a few little treats. . . . And I slipped some money into the old girl's hand—she took it as if it was her due—and promised to look in again tomorrow morning. . . . And what about you? Do you expect to be in for dinner?"

"I'm not sure yet, but I doubt it."

"How is Lognon?"

"The last I heard, he was still alive, but I've only just got back here."

"See you this evening, I hope."

"I hope so, too."

They never addressed each other by name, nor were they in the habit of exchanging endearments. What was the point, since both felt that, in many ways, they were one person?

He replaced the receiver and opened the door.

"Is Janvier there?"

"Coming, Chief."

And Maigret, now seated at his desk and rearranging his pipes, said:

"First of all, what news of Lognon?"

"I rang Bichat ten minutes ago. The matron is getting pretty fed up with us. . . . No change . . . The doctors weren't expecting any until tomorrow at the earliest. . . . He's still in a coma, and when he opens his eyes, he doesn't know where he is or what's happening to him, and he doesn't recognize anybody. . . ."

"Have you seen Marinette Augier's ex-fiancé?"

"I found him in his office, and he seemed scared to death that his father might find out that I was a policeman. . . . Apparently, his father is a holy terror, and has all the staff shivering in their shoes. . . . Jean-Claude is a bit of a dandy, but he seems pretty feeble and flabby. . . . He took me outside and went through a whole palaver in front of the receptionist, pretending that I was a customer. . . ."

"What does the firm make?"

"Metal tubing and all that sort of thing, in copper, iron, and steel. It's one of those great big sinister boxes that one sees so much around Avenue de la République and Boulevard Voltaire. He took me to a café a long way from his office. The afternoon papers mention the shooting and Lognon's injuries, but Marinette's name doesn't appear. Anyway, Jean-Claude hadn't seen a paper."

"Was he co-operative?"

"He's so terrified of his father, and of getting involved in anything that might cause trouble for him, that he would gladly have confessed all the sins of his youth, if I'd let him. . . . I told him that Marinette had suddenly vanished from her apartment, and that we needed her urgently as a witness. . . .

" 'You were engaged to her for nearly a year. . . .'

" 'Engaged? Well, that's placing it a bit high. . . .'

" 'Or a bit low, considering you spent a couple of nights a week in her apartment?'

"He was terribly upset that we should have found out about that.

" 'At any rate, if she's pregnant, it's not my fault. I haven't set eyes on her for over nine months. . . .'

"You can tell the sort he is, can't you, Chief? I asked him about the weekends.

" 'I daresay there were some places you liked better than others. . . . Have you a car?'

" 'Of course.'

" 'Did you used to go to the sea or just to the outskirts of Paris?'

" 'To the outskirts . . . Not always to the same place . . . We'd stop at some little inn or other, usually on the river, because Marinette was nuts about swimming and boating. She didn't care for hotels; they were too smart and sophisticated for her. To tell you the truth, she had rather low tastes. . . .'

"In the end, I managed to get half a dozen or so addresses out of him, places they'd been to more than once, the Auberge du Clou at Courcelles in the Vallée de Chevreuse, Chez Mélanie at Saint-Fargeau, midway between Corbeil and Melun, Félix et Félicie at Pomponne, on the Marne, not far from Lagny. . . . She had a specially soft spot for that particular bistro, because that's all it is, a country bistro with a couple of bedrooms above. It doesn't even have running water. . . .

"Then in Créguy, on the outskirts of Meaux, there's a sort of tea garden. He can't remember its name, only that the proprietor is deaf. . . . La Pie Qui Danse, right out in the country between Meulan and Apremont . . . And on one occasion they had lunch at the Coq Hardy in Bougival."

"Have you checked?"

"I thought it was better that I stay here, to co-ordinate all the information as it comes in. I could have phoned the various local police stations, but I was afraid they might bungle things, and frighten the girl into running away. . . . I know it's a bit irregular, since none of these places are in the Seine region, but I knew you were anxious to get things moving. . . ."

"Well?"

"I've sent a man to each district: Lourtie, Jamin, and Lagrume. . . ."

"Did you assign a car to each of them?"

"Yes," admitted Janvier, uneasily.

"So that's why, as Lucas has just informed me, there are no cars available?"

"I'm sorry. . . ."

"You did the right thing. . . . Any results yet?"

"Only at the Auberge du Clou. No news yet from nearer home . . . The others should be reporting in any time now. . . ."

Maigret smoked his pipe in silence, as if he had forgotten that the inspector was still there.

"Can I help you at all?"

"Not for the moment. Don't leave without letting me know. You'd better tell Lucas to stay on as well. . . ."

He was eager to get on with it. Ever since his long afternoon session with the Dutchman and his wife, he had had the feeling that someone was in danger, though he could not have said who.

Of course, the whole episode had been stage-managed for his benefit. No doubt the pictures on the walls were genuine, but he was sure that everything else he had seen and heard was phony.

"Put me through to the Aliens Office. . . ."

It took them about ten minutes to find out Madame Jonker's maiden name for him. Her original Christian name had not been Mireille, as he had supposed on account of her southern origin. No, Mirella Jonker had been christened with the much more common name Marcelle, Marcelle Maillant.

"Get me the Department of Criminal Investigation in Nice, will you? I'd like to speak to Superintendent Bastiani, if he's available. . . ."

Rather than sit doing nothing, he was pursuing, at random, every possible lead.

"Hello! Bastiani? How are you, old man? . . . Basking in the sunshine? Here we've had two solid days of rain. It didn't stop until this afternoon, and the sky is still overcast. . . . I say, could you do me a favor? . . . I'd be obliged if you could put a couple of your men on

to rooting among some of your old files. . . . If they find
nothing in your section, maybe they could try the Palais
de Justice. . . . It's about a woman named Marcelle Maillant. She was born in Nice, probably in the old quarter,
somewhere near Sainte-Réparate.

"She is thirty-four. She was formerly married to an
Englishman named Muir, a ball-bearings manufacturer
from Manchester. She lived in London for several years,
and there met and married a rich Dutchman, Norris
Jonker. They are now living in Paris. . . .

"She's a magnificent woman, the sort people turn
around to look at in the street. She's tall, dark, and well
groomed. Very much a woman of the world, but there's
something about her that doesn't ring true. . . . Do you
see what I'm getting at? There's something wrong somewhere, though I don't know what. . . . I can tell by the
way she looks at me. . . .

"Yes. It really is urgent. . . . There's something very
nasty brewing, I'm certain, and I want to prevent it if I
can. . . . By the way, did you, by any chance, know Lognon when you were in the Rue des Saussaies? Inspector
Grumpy, yes . . . He was shot last night. . . . He's not
dead, but it's touch and go. . . . There is a connection,
yes. . . . I'm puzzled as to exactly how she is involved,
and how deeply. . . . Your information may help me
there. . . .

"I'll be staying in my office, all night if necessary. . . ."

He was well aware that, knowing it to be connected
with the attempted murder of a colleague, Bastiani and
his men would go to work with a will. It would be a point
of honor with them.

For fully five minutes he sat slumped, as if in a dream,
then stretched out his hand to the telephone.

"I want a call put through to Scotland Yard. . . . Top priority . . . Inspector Pyke . . . Hang on a minute . . . No! Chief Inspector Pyke . . ."

They had met in France when the worthy Mr. Pyke had come to study the Department of Criminal Investigation's methods in general, and Maigret's in particular. He had been surprised to discover that Maigret had no method at all.

They had met twice more after that, in London, and had become good friends. Maigret had been told of Pyke's promotion some months ago.

Although it took no more than three minutes to get through to Scotland Yard, it took nearly ten to reach his friend, and they wasted a few more in mutual congratulations, Pyke speaking in bad French and Maigret in bad English.

"Maillant, yes . . . M for Maurice, A for Andrew . . ."

He had to spell out the names.

"Muir . . . M for Maurice again . . . U for Ursula . . ."

"Now that's a name I know. . . . Are you referring to Sir Herbert Muir? Of Manchester? He was knighted three years ago. . . ."

"The second husband's name is Norris Jonker. . . ."

He spelled that out, too, and went on to mention that the Dutchman had served in the British Army and had reached the rank of colonel.

"There may have been other men between the two marriages. . . . Apparently she lived in London for quite a while, and I can't see her living by herself. . . ."

Maigret was careful to add that his inquiries were connected with the attempted murder of a police officer, and Chief Inspector Pyke said solemnly:

"In this country, the criminal, whether a man or a

woman, would be sentenced to death. The murder of a policeman is always punishable by death. . . ."

Like Bastiani, he promised to call him back.

It was half past six. When Maigret opened the communicating door to the duty room, only four or five inspectors were still there.

"Nothing from Chez Mélanie in Saint-Fargeau, Chief. Nothing from the Coq Hardy or La Pie Qui Danse, either . . . I wasn't really expecting anything. . . . That leaves only the Marne region, now that we've drawn a blank in the Vallée de Chevreuse and the Seine. . . ."

Maigret was just about to return to his office when Inspector Chinquier burst into the room in a state of intense agitation.

"Is the Chief Superintendent in?"

Almost before the question was out of his mouth, he saw him.

"I've got news for you. . . . I decided to come myself, rather than telephone. . . ."

"Come into my office."

"I've brought a witness. . . . I've left him outside in the waiting room, in case you should want to question him yourself. . . ."

"First of all, sit down and tell me about it."

"Do you mind if I take off my coat? I've been rushing around so much today that I'm sweating like a pig. Well, here goes! In accordance with your wishes, the men of the Eighteenth Arrondissement have been going through Avenue Junot and all the streets nearby with a fine-tooth comb. Except for old Maclet, they couldn't find anyone at first who was able to help. Then out of the blue I received information I judged to be of the utmost significance. . . .

"That particular building had already been visited this afternoon. The concierge had been questioned, and also those tenants who were there at the time, not many, women mostly, because the men were out at work. . . .

"I'm speaking of a block of apartments right at the top of the avenue. . . .

"Just as one of my colleagues arrived there for the second time—less than an hour ago—a man was going into the lodge to collect his mail. His name is Langeron, and he's a door-to-door salesman of vacuum cleaners. . . . I've brought him with me. . . .

"He's not the most cheerful of men, being more used to having the door slammed in his face than to being received with open arms. . . . He lives alone in rooms on the third floor. He works irregular hours, in the hope of discovering the most favorable time for calling on his potential customers. . . .

"Most of the time he cooks his own meals, but whenever he has a successful day, he treats himself to a meal in a restaurant. . . . That's what happened last night. Between six and eight in the evening, when most people are at home, he sold two vacuum cleaners, and, after having an apéritif in a brasserie in Place de Clichy, he had a huge meal in a little restaurant in Rue Caulaincourt.

"A little before ten, he returned to Avenue Junot, carrying his demonstration model, and saw a parked car outside the Dutchman's house. It was a yellow Jaguar, and he was struck by the license number, because the letters TT were painted in red.

"He had gone only a few yards when the door opened. . . ."

"Is he sure it was the door of the Jonkers' house?"

"He knows all the houses on the Avenue Junot like the back of his hand, having, needless to say, tried to sell a vacuum cleaner to practically everyone on it. . . . Now listen to this. . . . Two men came out, supporting a third, who was so drunk he couldn't stand upright. . . .

"When the two men, who were virtually carrying the other man to the car, caught sight of Langeron, they looked as if they were about to return indoors, but then one of them said, crossly:

" 'Come on, you idiot, move! You ought to be ashamed of yourself, getting into this state!' "

"Did they drive away with him?"

"Just a minute. That's not all. In the first place, my friend, the vacuum-cleaner salesman, says that the man who spoke had a strong English accent. . . . And furthermore, he says, the drunk wasn't wearing any shoes or socks. . . . Apparently, his bare feet were dragging along the pavement. . . . He was bundled into the back seat, followed by one of the two men. The other took the wheel. And the car drove off at high speed. . . .

"Would you like to see my witness?"

Maigret hesitated, haunted by the conviction that time was getting very short.

"Take him next door and have him dictate a statement. Make certain he leaves nothing out. One can never be sure that some quite trivial detail may not turn out to be important. . . ."

"What shall I do with him after that?"

"Come and see me again when you've finished."

The previous night, at this very same hour, he had been leaning on young Bauche, nicknamed Jeannot, and

it had been one o'clock in the morning before he had
wrested a confession from him, which had enabled him
to arrest Gaston Nouveau.

He was beginning to fear that tonight, also, there
would be a light burning in his office until God knows
what time. It was unusual for him to be working so late
two nights in succession. There was almost always an
interval between cases, and, paradoxically enough, there
was nothing like a prolonged interval to make Maigret
feel thoroughly restless and disgruntled.

"Get me Motor Vehicle Registrations. . . . And hurry!"

He could not remember ever having seen a yellow
Jaguar, a color that was, anyway, uncommon for a British car. The letters TT indicated that the car had been
brought to France by a foreign owner who intended to
stay for only a short while, and was therefore not required
to pay any import duty.

"Who in your department deals with TT registrations?
. . . Rorive? . . . He's not there? . . . Everybody has gone
home? . . . Well, you're still there, aren't you? . . . Listen to me, son . . . you'll just have to manage on your
own. It's absolutely vital. . . . You can do one of two
things: go into Rorive's office and look up the information I require, or call him at his home and tell him to
come back at once. I don't give a damn if he is in the
middle of dinner. . . . Understood? . . . It's about a
Jaguar . . . yes, a Jaguar. . . .

"It was seen being driven in Paris as recently as yesterday evening. . . . It's yellow, and fitted with TT plates.
. . . No, I don't know the number. That would be too
much to hope for. . . . But there can't be all that many
yellow Jaguars with TT plates in Paris. . . .

"Put your skates on, and as soon as you have the information, call me here at the Quai. . . . I want the name of the owner, his address, and the date of his arrival in France. . . . I hope it won't be long before I hear from you. . . . Oh! and if you have to disturb Rorive, apologize to him for me. . . . I hope to be able to repay him sometime. . . . Tell him it's a lead to the fellow who shot Lognon. . . . Yes, the inspector from the Eighteenth Arrondissement . . ."

He went across and opened the communicating door, and called Janvier in.

"Nothing yet from the Marne district?"

"Not yet. Maybe Lagrume has had a flat tire. . . ."

"What's the time?"

"Seven o'clock."

"I'm thirsty. . . . Have them send up a few beers. . . . And, while you're about it, you may as well order some sandwiches."

"For how many?"

"I've no idea. . . . A pile of sandwiches . . ."

With his hands behind his back, he paced up and down for a while, then once again picked up the telephone receiver.

"Could you get me my wife, please. . . ."

To tell her that he would certainly not be home for dinner.

No sooner had he hung up than the telephone bell rang.

Hastily, he picked up the receiver.

"Hello! . . . Yes . . . Bastiani . . . So it turned out to be easier than you thought? . . . A stroke of luck? . . . Good! . . . Go ahead. . . ."

He sat down at his desk, notebook in hand, and picked up a pencil.

"What name did you say? . . . Stanley Hobson . . .

What's that? . . . A long story? . . . Well, cut it as short as you can, but don't leave anything out. . . . Of course not, my dear fellow . . . It's just that I'm a bit on edge this evening. . . . I have a feeling that we need to move fast. . . . I'm plagued by the vision of a barefoot drunk. . . . Okay. I'm listening."

The incident went back sixteen years. It concerned a man by the name of Stanley Hobson, who was staying in Nice at one of the big hotels on the Promenade des Anglais. On a tip from Scotland Yard, he was arrested and charged with a number of thefts of jewelry from villas in Antibes and Cannes, and also from one of the rooms in the hotel where he was staying.

At the time of his arrest he was with a girl who was not quite eighteen, and who had been his mistress for several weeks past.

They had arrested her at the same time. Both were held for questioning for several days. Their hotel room had been searched, and so had the girl's mother's apartment in the old quarter. The girl, it seemed, had earned her living by selling flowers in the market.

No jewelry was found. For lack of evidence the couple were released, and two days later they had crossed the frontier into Italy.

In Nice, nothing more was ever heard of Hobson, or of Marcelle Maillant, for it was indeed she who was the girl in the case.

"Do you happen to know what became of her mother?"

"For several years now she's been living in a comfortable apartment on Rue Saint-Sauveur on a private income. I've sent one of my men to see her, but he hasn't got back yet. . . . I presume she gets an allowance from her daughter. . . ."

"Thanks, Bastiani. You'll be hearing from me again soon, I hope."

The wheels were beginning to turn, as Maigret was fond of saying, and at a time like this he could have wished that all the offices in the building were manned night and day.

"Come in here a minute, Lucas. . . . I want you to go down to Licensed Rentals. . . . I hope you won't find everyone gone. . . . Make a note of this name . . . Stanley Hobson. . . . According to Bastiani, he must, by now, be between forty-five and forty-eight years old. . . . I don't have a description, but, fifteen years ago or more, he was suspected of being involved in a number of international jewel robberies, and at that time Scotland Yard issued his description to every police force in Europe. . . .

"If necessary, go upstairs and see if they've got anything on him in Records. . . ."

When Lucas had gone, Maigret looked reproachfully at the telephone, as if he felt it was letting him down by not ringing incessantly. Then there was a knock on his door. It was Chinquier.

"Here you are, Chief Superintendent . . . here is Langeron's statement, duly typed and signed. He says can he go and have some dinner. Do you really not want to see him?"

Maigret was satisfied with a mere glimpse of the man through the half-open door. He looked very ordinary and insignificant.

"Tell him he's welcome to go out to dinner, but that he's to be sure to come back here afterward. I don't know when I may need him, if at all, but there are too many people in this case already scattered about all over the place. . . ."

"What should I do next?"

"Aren't you hungry? Do you never have dinner?"

"I'd like to help in any way I can. . . ."

"The best thing would be for you to go back to your own office, so that you can keep me informed of any new developments in your district."

"Are you hoping for a breakthrough?"

"If I weren't, I'd go straight home to my wife, and we'd have dinner together and watch television. . . ."

The waiter from the Brasserie Dauphine was just putting down a tray laden with sandwiches and glasses of beer when the telephone rang.

"Splendid! . . . Congratulations . . . Ed? . . . Just Ed? . . . An American? . . . Yes, I see. . . . Even their presidents are familiarly known by diminutives. . . . Ed Gollan . . . Two l's? . . . Do you have his address? . . . What? What's that? . . ."

Maigret's brow clouded over. The man in question was the owner of the yellow Jaguar.

"Are you sure it's the only one of its kind in Paris? . . . Good . . . Thanks, old man . . . I'll follow it up at once, but I wish he was staying anywhere but at the Ritz. . . ."

Once more, he looked in on the inspectors' room.

"I hope there are some cars left in the forecourt, because I want two of you to go and get hold of one. . . ."

"Two cars have just driven in."

A few seconds later, he was on the telephone again.

"Is that the Ritz? . . . Would you get me the head porter, please, mademoiselle. . . . Hello! Is that the head porter? Is that you, Pierre? . . . Maigret speaking . . ."

Maigret had more than once conducted an investigation at the Ritz, in the Place Vendôme, one of the most select hotels, if not *the* most select, in Paris, and had always proceeded with the utmost discretion.

"The Chief Superintendent, that's right. . . . Now listen carefully, and don't mention any names. . . . At this time of the evening, the foyer must be crowded. . . . Have you anyone staying there by the name of Gollan, Ed Gollan? . . ."

"Do you mind holding on a moment? I think I'd better get this call transferred to one of the booths. . . ."

No sooner was this done than the head porter was able to give Maigret the information he wanted:

"Yes, he is here. . . . He stays here quite often. . . . He's an American from San Francisco. He travels a lot, and comes to Paris three or four times a year. . . . As a rule, he stays about three weeks. . . ."

"How old a man is he?"

"Forty-eight . . . Not one of your business types at all . . . More of an intellectual, I'd say. . . . According to his passport, he's an art critic, and I've heard it said that he has an international reputation as an expert. . . . He's entertained the director of the Louvre on several occasions, and all the big picture dealers call on him when he's here. . . ."

"Is he in his suite now?"

"Let me see . . . what time is it? . . . Half past seven? . . . He's probably in the bar. . . ."

"Would you check on that? . . . As discreetly as you can, of course . . ."

Another pause.

"Yes, he's there. . . ."

"Alone?"

"He's got a good-looking woman with him."

"Is she staying in the hotel?"

"She's not quite the type. . . . It's not the first time she's had a drink with him in the bar. . . . Later, he'll probably take her out somewhere for dinner."

"Could you let me know as soon as they show any sign of leaving?"

"I'll be glad to, but I won't be able to stop them. . . ."

"Don't worry about that. . . . Just give me a call. . . . And thanks!"

He called Lucas into his office.

"Listen carefully. This is urgent, and you'll have to handle it with great discretion. I want you and another inspector to go to the Ritz right away. Tell the head porter I sent you, and ask him if Ed Gollan is still in the bar. If he is, as I'm hoping he will be, leave your colleague in the foyer and, very discreetly, go and have a word with Gollan and his companion. . . .

"Don't show your badge, or announce yourself in a loud voice as a police officer. . . . Just tell him it's about his car, and that we want the answers to one or two questions. Insist on his coming with you. . . ."

"What about the woman? Is she to come, too?"

"Not unless she's tall and dark and very beautiful, and answers to the name of Mirella. . . ."

Lucas cast a longing glance at the still-frosted glasses of beer, then turned and went out without a word.

"Remember, speed is of the essence. . . . Get there as fast as you can. . . ."

The beer was good, but Maigret was not tempted by the sandwiches. He was too agitated to eat. Nothing seemed to hang together in this case. No sooner did he evolve a theory than new evidence turned up to belie it.

And, except for the mysterious Stanley Hobson, everyone concerned seemed, on the face of it, to be thoroughly respectable.

Having given the matter some thought, he decided to telephone Manessi, the appraiser, at his home.

"It's me again, yes. . . . I hope you're not in the middle of a party. . . . You are? . . . Then I'll be brief. . . . Does the name Gollan mean anything to you? . . . One of the most respected of American art experts . . ."

As he listened to what Manessi had to tell him, he sighed more than once.

"Yes . . . Yes . . . I might have known. . . . Just one more question . . . I was told this afternoon that the real connoisseurs of painting often prefer to resell under the counter, so to speak. That's right, is it? . . . Naturally, I won't ask you to name names. . . . No, the case I'm working on has no connection with works of art, or if it has, I don't know what the connection is. . . . One last word . . . is it conceivable that a man like Norris Jonker would have any fakes in his collection? . . ."

Manessi, at the other end of the line, laughted heartily.

"It's just about as likely as looking for fakes in the Louvre. . . . Admittedly, there are those who claim that the Mona Lisa in the Louvre is a copy. . . ."

The door burst open, and Janvier appeared, looking highly excited, indeed radiant. He could hardly wait for Maigret to hang up.

"I'm much obliged to you. . . . Now you can go back to your guests. . . . I hope I'm wrong, but I think I may have to come back to you. . . ."

Janvier could not contain his news for another second. He exploded:

"We've done it, Chief! . . . She's been found. . . ."

"Marinette?"

"Yes . . . Lagrume is driving her back to Paris. . . . It wasn't a flat tire that held him up; it's just that it took him a long time to find the inn, Félix et Félicie. It's on the far side of Pomponne, at the end of a dirt road that leads nowhere."

"Has he got anything out of her?"

"She swears she knows nothing. When she heard the shots, she thought immediately of Lognon. She was afraid they might be gunning for her as well."

"Why?"

"She didn't offer any explanation. . . . She made no difficulties about coming back with Lagrume, not after he'd shown her his badge, that is. . . ."

They would be arriving at the Quai des Orfèvres within the hour. Before that, all being well, Ed Gollan would have arrived, fuming, no doubt, and threatening to complain to his embassy. It was amazing the number of people who were prepared to bother their embassies!

"Hello! . . . Yes . . . Chief Inspector Pyke, my dear fellow! Yes, it's I in person. . . ."

The recently promoted Scotland Yard Chief Inspector said his say in a leisurely manner, sounding as if he were reading from a prepared text, and, whenever anything of importance came up, he repeated the words.

And a great deal of his information was extremely important. For instance, that the marriage between Mirella and her first husband, Herbert Muir, had lasted only two years. The young woman had been sued for divorce as the guilty party, and the co-respondent, to use the English term, had been none other than Stanley Hobson.

Not only had the pair been caught *in flagrante delicto*, in the somewhat dubious district of Manchester where

Hobson was living at the time, but it was further established that, throughout the two-year duration of the marriage, Mirella and Hobson had never ceased to meet.

"I have not yet been able to find out whether Hobson was in London at all during the intervening years. I hope to be able to tell you more about that tomorrow. I'm putting two of my men onto the job of having a word with some people in Soho who know everything that goes on in the criminal fraternity. . . .

"Oh! there's one other thing. . . . Hobson is best known by his nickname, Bald Stan. At the age of twenty-three or twenty-four, following some illness or other, he lost all his hair, and his eyebrows and eyelashes. . . ."

Maigret, who was feeling overheated, went across and opened the window a little. He was just finishing one of the glasses of beer when he heard, outside in the corridor, someone speaking in French with an American accent. He couldn't hear the words, but it was clear from the tone of the voice that the speaker was beside himself with anger.

Accordingly, Maigret, assuming his most friendly, affable, and smiling manner, opened the door, and said:

"Please come in, Monsieur Gollan, and forgive me for putting you to all this trouble. . . ."

7 / Mirella's Choice

Ed Gollan had brown crew-cut hair. Even though the sky was overcast and the air cold, he had not bothered to put on a coat, and his lightweight suit, with its unpadded shoulders, made him look even taller than he was.

In spite of his fury, he was not at a loss for words, and his French was both fluent and grammatical.

"This gentleman," he said, pointing to Lucas, "came on the scene at a most inopportune moment. It was embarrassing not only for me, but also for the lady who was with me . . . ."

Maigret spoke quietly to Lucas, who left the room.

"I'm extremely sorry, Monsieur Gollan. You mustn't think too badly of him, though. He was only doing his job."

The art critic got the point.

"I presume it concerns my car?"

"You are the owner of a yellow Jaguar, are you not?"

"I was."

"What do you mean?"

"That this morning I went in person to the divisional

police headquarters in the First Arrondissement to report that it had been stolen."

"Where were you yesterday evening, Monsieur Gollan?"

"With the Mexican consul, at his home on Boulevard des Italiens."

"Did you dine there?"

"Yes. With a party of about a dozen people."

"Were you still there at ten o'clock?"

"Not only was I there at ten, I was still there at two in the morning. You can check, if you like."

Noticing the tray loaded with glasses of beer and sandwiches, he looked surprised.

"I'd be obliged if you would tell me right away . . ."

"One moment. I am pressed for time myself, more pressed than you are, believe me, but it's essential that we take things in their proper order. Did you leave your car on the Boulevard des Italiens?"

"No. You know as well as I do that it's virtually impossible to find a parking space there."

"Where was it when you saw it last?"

"In the Place Vendôme, where a certain amount of parking space is reserved for residents of the Ritz. I only had a few hundred yards' walk to get to my friend's house."

"Were you away from his apartment at any time during the evening?"

"No."

"Did you receive a telephone call?"

He hesitated, apparently surprised that Maigret should know.

"From a woman, yes."

"From someone whom you would no doubt prefer not to name? The call was from Madame Jonker, wasn't it?"

"It might have been. As it happens, I do know the Jonkers."

"When you got back to the hotel, didn't you notice that your car was no longer there?"

"I used the Rue Cambon entrance, as most of the residents do."

"Do you know Stanley Hobson?"

"It is not my intention, Chief Superintendent, to allow myself to be interrogated until I know what this is all about."

"It concerns some friends of yours who happen to be in trouble."

"What friends?"

"Norris Jonker, for one . . . I presume you have sold pictures to him, and perhaps bought from him as well? . . ."

"I'm not a picture dealer. . . . I am occasionally commissioned by museums and private collectors to find them a painting by a specific artist, representing a specific period in his development, and of greater or lesser importance in the canon of his works. . . . If, in the course of my travels, I happen to learn that a painting of the right sort is on the market, I merely pass on the information to those concerned. . . ."

"Without taking any commission?"

"That's no business of yours. It's between me and the Internal Revenue Service."

"I presume I can take it for granted that you have no idea who stole your car. Did you have the key on the dashboard?"

"It was in the glove compartment. I'm so absent-minded that if I carried it on me, I'd be sure to lose it."

Maigret was listening with half an ear for sounds in the corridor. He seemed to be asking questions at random, without any real sense of purpose.

Well, Gollan was the first fish in his net, wasn't he?

"I presume I am now free to rejoin the lady I have invited to dine with me?"

"Not quite yet, I'm afraid. I may need you again later. . . ."

Maigret had heard footsteps, then the opening and shutting of a door, followed by the sound of a woman's voice in the adjoining office. This was the night of the clicking doors, or so it came to be called later.

"Janvier, would you mind coming into my office for a minute. It would be discourteous to leave Monsieur Gollan by himself. We've already caused him to miss his dinner, so if he would care for a sandwich . . ."

The few inspectors whom Maigret had asked to stay on, including Lagrume, who was bursting with pride at the success of his mission, were all looking with interest at a charming young woman wearing a blue tailored suit, and she, in her turn, was taking note of her surroundings.

"You're Chief Superintendent Maigret, aren't you? I've seen your picture in the papers. Please tell me at once, is he dead?"

"No, Mademoiselle Augier. He is still on the critical list, but the doctors hope to be able to save him."

"Was he the one who told you about me?"

"He's in no condition to speak, and won't be for hours yet, perhaps not for two or three days. I'd be obliged if you would come with me."

He led her into a little side office and shut the door.

"I think you will understand what I mean when I say that we have no time to lose. That's why I won't ask you now to tell me all you know in detail. There will be time enough for that later. I just want to ask you a few questions. Was it through you that Inspector Lognon learned of the strange things that were going on in the house opposite?"

"No. I hadn't noticed a thing, except that there was often a light on in the studio at night. . . ."

"Where did you meet?"

"In the street, one evening, when I was on my way home from work. He told me he'd found out that the apartment I was living in was an ideal place from which to keep watch on someone, and asked if he might spend the next two or three nights looking out of my sitting-room window. He showed me his police badge and identity card. I wasn't too happy about it, and even thought of calling the police station."

"What made you change your mind?"

"He seemed so miserable. He told me he'd always been dogged by bad luck, but, if only I would help him, all that would change, because he was on the track of something really big. . . ."

"Did he say what?"

"Not the first night."

"Did you watch with him, that first night?"

"For a time, yes, in the dark. The curtains of the studio opposite didn't quite meet, and from time to time we could see a man moving across the gap, holding a palette and paintbrush."

"Was he dressed all in white? With a turban wound round his head?"

"Yes. I laughed, and said he looked for all the world like a ghostly apparition."

"Did you ever see him at work?"

"Once. On that particular night, he had set up his easel in a position where we could see it, and he was painting away furiously. . . ."

"How does one paint furiously?"

"I don't know, but he gave the impression of being a man possessed."

"Did you ever see anyone else in the studio?"

"A woman. She was undressing, or I should say, he almost tore the clothes off her. . . ."

"Was she tall and dark?"

"It wasn't Madame Jonker. I know *her* by sight."

"Have you ever seen Monsieur Jonker?"

"Not in the studio. The only other person I ever saw there was an elderly bald man."

"What happened last night, exactly?"

"I went to bed early as usual. I come home from work very tired, especially when the salon stays open later than usual because of some fashionable ball or gala performance."

"Was Lognon in the living room?"

"Yes. We got on very well together in the end. . . . He never tried to make a pass at me, and he was always very kind, in a fatherly sort of way. Sometimes he'd bring me some chocolates or a bunch of violets as a thank-you present. . . ."

"Were you asleep at ten o'clock?"

"I was in bed, but I hadn't yet fallen asleep. I was reading the paper. . . . He knocked on my door. . . . He seemed wildly excited. He told me there had been a new development, that they had just abducted the painter, but it had all happened so quickly that he had had no chance of getting downstairs in time. . . .

" 'I'd better stay here a little longer. . . . At least one of the men is almost sure to come back. . . .'

"He returned to his post at the window, and I went to sleep. . . . I was awakened by the sound of shots. . . . I looked out of my window. . . . Then I leaned forward and saw a body lying on the pavement. . . . I hadn't, at that stage, decided what to do, but I began to get dressed. . . . The concierge came up and told me what had happened. . . ."

"Why did you run away?"

"I was afraid the criminals might know who he was and what he was up to in the building, in which case they might have it in for me as well. . . . I didn't know where I was going. . . . I just didn't stop to think. . . ."

"Did you take a taxi?"

"No. I walked as far as Place de Clichy, and went into a café that was still open. I stayed there for a while, during which time I was examined from head to foot by all the prostitutes in the place. . . . Then I remembered an inn where I used occasionally to go and stay with a friend, some time back. . . ."

"Yes, with Jean-Claude . . ."

"Was he the one who told you?"

"See here, mademoiselle, everything that concerns you interests me, and I should be happy to hear the full story of your adventure. But I have a feeling that there are more urgent matters to be dealt with. . . . I'd be greatly obliged if you'd be good enough to wait for me in the inspectors' duty room. I'll show you the way. . . . In the meantime, Inspector Janvier will be pleased to take down your statement in writing. . . ."

"Lognon wasn't mistaken, then?"

"No! Lognon knows his job, and seldom jumps to the wrong conclusion. . . . As he told you, he's been unlucky, one way and another. . . . Either the ground is cut from under his feet, or he gets himself shot just when he's on the point of making his mark. . . . Come with me!"

He left her in the adjoining office and returned to his own to find Janvier waiting for him.

"I'd be grateful if you would take down the young lady's statement."

At this, Gollan, who had been seated, sprang to his feet.

"You don't mean to say you've brought her here?"

"We're not talking about your friend, Monsieur Gollan. This one is a real lady. . . . Do you still maintain that you've never met Stanley Hobson, better known as 'Bald Stan'?"

"I don't have to answer that."

"As you please . . . Sit down. . . . I'm about to make a telephone call. You may find it helpful. . . . Hello! . . . Get me Monsieur Jonker, will you? Norris Jonker, on Avenue Junot . . .

"Hello! . . . Monsieur Jonker? . . . Maigret speaking. . . . Since I left your house, I have found the answers to a number of the questions I put to you. . . . The real answers, if you get my meaning . . .

"For instance, I have Monsieur Gollan with me, here in my office, and he's none too happy about it, especially since he still hasn't found his missing car . . . a yellow Jaguar. . . . The one that was seen outside your house at ten o'clock last night, and which drove away with your lodger, among others, inside. . . .

"Your lodger . . . That's right. . . . And in very poor shape, it seems . . . wearing no shoes or socks . . .

"Now, listen carefully, Monsieur Jonker. . . . I could, if I so wished, have you arrested tonight or tomorrow morning on charges relating to certain illegal activities, the details of which are more familiar to you than to me. . . . I'd better warn you, in any case, that there is a police guard on your house. . . .

"I am asking you to come and see me here at once, accompanied by Madame Jonker, so that we may continue our conversation of this afternoon. . . . If your wife is inclined to make difficulties, tell her we know the whole of her history. . . . It's possible that, in addition to Monsieur Gollan, she may meet another friend here, a man generally known as 'Bald Stan.'

"That's enough, Monsieur Jonker! . . . For the present, I'm doing the talking. . . . Your turn will come very soon now. . . . I daresay it is embarrassing to be mixed up in a case of forgery, but it is surely less so than if I had charged you with being an accessory to murder. . . .

"I am convinced that the attack on Inspector Lognon came as a surprise to you, and probably to Monsieur Gollan, as well. . . . But I'm very much afraid that plans are afoot for another murder, which concerns you more nearly, since the intended victim is the man who for some time lived in your house, virtually as a prisoner. . . . Where is he? . . . Where has he been taken, and by whom? Tell me that. . . . No, not when you get here . . . not in half an hour's time . . . Now, Monsieur Jonker, do you hear me?"

He could hear the murmur of a woman's voice. Mirella must be leaning over her husband's shoulder. What was she advising him to do?

"I swear to you, Chief Superintendent . . ."

"And I repeat that there is no time to lose. . . ."

"Hold on! . . . I don't know the number offhand. . . . I'll have to look it up in my book. . . ."

At this point, Mirella openly intervened:

"He's looking up the address, Monsieur Maigret. . . . The man's name is Mario de Lucia. He has a furnished apartment somewhere near the Champs-Elysées. . . . Ah! here's my husband. . . ."

Jonker read out:

"Mario de Lucia, 27B Rue de Berri . . . I have entrusted Federigo to his care. . . ."

"I take it Federigo is the painter to whom you lent your studio?"

"Yes . . . Federigo Palestri . . ."

"I shall be expecting you, Monsieur Jonker. . . . And be sure to bring your wife with you. . . ."

Maigret did not spare a glance for the American art critic. He had already picked up the receiver again.

"Get me the superintendent of the Eighth Arrondissement. . . . Hello! . . . Who is that speaking? . . . Dubois? I want you to go to an address I shall read out to you. . . . Take three or four men with you. . . . Yes, I did say three or four. . . . I want you all armed, because the man is dangerous. . . . The address is 27B Rue de Berri. The man—his name is Mario de Lucia—has a furnished apartment in the building. . . . If he's at home, as I think he will be, arrest him. Yes, in spite of the lateness of the hour. . . .

"You'll find another man being held prisoner there. His name is Federigo Palestri. I want both these men brought here as soon as possible. . . . I repeat, be very

careful. . . . Mario de Lucia is armed with a .763 Mauser.
. . . If he hasn't got it on him, find it! . . ."

He turned to Ed Gollan.

"You see, monsieur, it would be unwise of you to make
difficulties. . . . It's taken me a long time to work it all
out, because I know very little about the traffic in paintings, genuine or faked. . . . And besides, your friend
Jonker is a gentleman who is not easily thrown off balance. . . ."

The telephone rang and, once again, he grabbed the
receiver.

"Yes . . . Hello! . . . Is that you, Lucas? . . . Where are
you? . . . Quai de la Tournelle? . . . Hôtel de la Tournelle?
. . . I see. . . . He's having dinner in a nearby bistro? . . .
No, not alone . . . Get a couple of the local inspectors
to go along with you. After all, we can't be sure he isn't
the one who likes playing around with large-caliber guns.
It would surprise me, but it would be just poor Lognon's
luck. . . ."

He went across to the door communicating with the
inspectors' duty room and opened it.

"I'd like some more chilled beer sent up. . . ."

He returned to his seat and began filling his pipe.

"Well! There it is, Monsieur Gollan! . . . I hope your
painter friend is still alive. I don't know Mario de Lucia
personally, but I daresay we have him on our books
under one name or another. . . . If not, we shall get in
touch with the Italian police. . . . It shouldn't be more
than a few minutes before we get some definite news.
You might as well admit it, you're as worried as I am."

"I refuse to say anything, except in the presence of my
lawyer, Maître Spangler. His telephone number is Odéon
18.24. . . . No, that's not right. . . ."

"It's of no consequence, Monsieur Gollan. . . . As things are at present, your statement can wait. It's a pity a man like you should have allowed himself to become entangled in this business, and I hope Maître Spangler will be able to put forward sound arguments in your defense."

The beer had not yet arrived before the telephone rang again.

"Yes . . . Dubois?"

He listened for some time without saying a word.

"Right! . . . Thanks . . . It's no fault of yours. . . . You'd better report direct to the D.P.P. . . . I'll look in there later. . . ."

Maigret got up, avoiding the unspoken question in the eyes of the American, who had turned pale.

"Has something happened? I swear to you that if . . ."

"Sit down and be quiet."

He went next door and beckoned to Janvier, who was engaged in typing Marinette Augier's statement, to join him in the corridor.

"Anything wrong, Chief?"

"I don't yet know exactly what has happened. . . . The painter of those graffiti has been found hanging from the lavatory chain in the bathroom where he was being kept prisoner. Mario de Lucia has disappeared. . . . You'll probably find a file on him upstairs. . . . Put out a general alert to all railway stations, airports, and frontier posts. . . ."

"What about Marinette?"

"She can wait. . . ."

A man and a woman were coming up the stairs, discreetly followed by a uniformed policeman from the Eighteenth Arrondissement.

"I'd be obliged if you would wait in that room there, Madame Jonker. . . ."

The two women, who knew one another by sight but had never before met face to face, eyed each other with interest.

"And you, Monsieur Jonker, please come with me. . . ."

He led him into the little side office where he had interviewed Marinette Augier.

"Please take a seat. . . ."

"Have you found him?"

"Yes."

"Alive?"

The Dutchman had lost both his rosy complexion and his self-assurance. In the course of a few hours, he had become an old man.

"Has Lucia . . . killed him?"

"He was found hanged in the bathroom. . . ."

"I always said it would end badly. . . ."

"To whom?"

"To Mirella . . . and others . . . But especially to my wife . . ."

"How much do you know about her?"

It was hard for him to make the admission, but with bowed head he managed it.

"Everything, I think. . . ."

"Do you know about Nice and Stanley Hobson?"

"Yes."

"And that he was the co-respondent in the divorce suit brought by Herbert Muir in Manchester?"

"Yes."

"Did you meet her in London?"

"At a country house near London, where I was staying with friends . . . She was very popular in her own particular set. . . ."

"And you fell in love with her? . . . Was it you who proposed marriage?"

"Yes."

"Did you know about her, even then?"

"You may find this hard to believe, though a fellow countryman of mine would understand. . . . I hired a private detective to find out more about her. . . . I discovered that she and Hobson, nicknamed 'Bald Stan,' had lived together for some years. I also discovered that the British police had only managed once to make a charge stick, and that he had served a two-year sentence. . . .

"By the time he found her again, in Manchester, she was married to Muir. . . . When she moved to London, they had ceased to live together, but he used to visit her at intervals, to extort money. . . ."

There was a knock at the door.

"Would you like some beer, Chief?"

"You, Monsieur Jonker, I daresay, would prefer a brandy. . . . I'm sorry I can't offer you your favorite brand. Send someone to fetch the bottle of *fine champagne* from the cupboard in my office. . . ."

Soon they were alone together once more. The spirits, swallowed at one gulp, had brought a little of the color back to the Dutchman's cheeks.

"You see, Chief Superintendent, I can't live without her. . . . Falling in love at my age is a very dangerous thing. She told me that Hobson was blackmailing her, but said that he was prepared to be bought off if the price was right, and I believed her. . . . I paid. . . ."

"How did the picture racket start?"

"You'll find this hard to believe, but then, you are not a collector. . . ."

"I collect people. . . ."

"I wonder how you would classify me in your collection. . . . As a fool, perhaps? . . . Since you have been making inquiries about me, you will undoubtedly have been told that I am genuinely an expert on the paintings of a specific period. . . . When one has immersed oneself, for so many years, in one particular branch of learning, one is bound to acquire a great deal of specialized knowledge, isn't that so?

"I am often asked for my opinion on this painting or that. . . . And it is enough that a picture formed part of my collection for a time for it to be accepted without question. . . ."

"A hallmark of authenticity, in fact. . . ."

"The same is true of any major collection. . . . As I told you when you came to my house, I sometimes sell a picture in order to replace it with a finer and rarer example of the artist's work. Once one has started, it is difficult to stop. . . . Once, I made a mistake. . . ."

His voice sounded listless, as if he no longer cared what happened to him.

"The painting in question was a Van Gogh, no less. Not one of those I inherited from my father, but one I bought through an agent. I could have sworn it was genuine. . . . I kept it for a while in my drawing room. . . . A South American collector offered me a sum so large for it that it would have enabled me to replace it with a picture that I had had my eye on for a long time. . . .

"The sale was concluded. . . . A few months later, the man Gollan, whom I knew only by name, came to see me."

"How long ago was this?"

"About a year ago . . . He mentioned the Van Gogh, which he happened to have seen in the home of the Venezuelan purchaser, and was able to convince me that the painting was a clever fake. . . .

" 'I didn't say a word to the owner,' he stated. . . . 'It would make it most unpleasant for you—wouldn't it? —if anyone were to find out that you had passed on a fake. . . . Others who had bought pictures from you might start feeling uneasy. Indeed, it would throw doubt on your entire collection.'

"I repeat, you are not a collector. . . . You can't possibly imagine what a fearful blow this was to me. . . .

"Gollan came to see me again. . . . One day, he announced that he had found the artist who had forged the Van Gogh. . . . He said he was a pleasant young man, who claimed to be able to imitate, equally convincingly, the style of Manet, Renoir, or Vlaminck."

"Was your wife present on that occasion?"

"I don't remember. . . . It's possible that I may have told her about it afterward. . . . Possibly she urged me to agree to his proposition. . . . Possibly I would have agreed anyway. . . . I am known as a rich man, but wealth is a relative term. Though I have the means to buy some pictures, there are others that are beyond my resources, however much I may want to own them. . . . Do you understand?"

"I think I understand this much: it was essential that you retain the forgeries for a while, to establish their authenticity beyond dispute."

"That's about it. . . . I would hang one or two forgeries among my own pictures, and . . ."

"One moment! At what stage did you actually meet Palestri?"

"A month or two later . . . I had already sold two of his works, with Gollan acting as agent. . . . Gollan preferred, if he could, to sell to South American collectors or obscure little out-of-the-way museums. . . .

"Palestri was giving him a lot of trouble. . . . He was a sort of crazy genius, with an insatiable sexual appetite. . . . You could see that, when you went into his bedroom, couldn't you? . . ."

"Light began to dawn when I saw your wife standing at the easel. . . ."

"We had no choice but to try to put you off the scent. . . ."

"When and how did you discover that someone was taking an interest in the goings-on in your house?"

"It wasn't I who noticed it; it was Hobson. . . ."

"Hobson had come back into your wife's life?"

"They both swear not. . . . Hobson just happened to be a friend of Gollan's. . . . It was he who put him on to Palestri. . . . Do I make myself clear? . . ."

"Yes."

"I was trapped. . . . I agreed to let him work in the studio, where no one would think of looking for him. . . . He slept in the room you went into. . . . He was quite prepared to stay indoors, provided we procured women for him. . . . Painting and women were his only passions. . . ."

"I was told that he 'painted furiously.' "

"Yes . . . Two or three fine originals would be propped up in front of him. He would circle around them like a matador with a bull, and a few hours or a few days later, he would come up with a painting so akin in feeling and texture to the original that everyone was taken in. . . .

"It wasn't very pleasant to have him living on the premises. . . ."

"You mean on account of his insatiable appetite for women?"

"And his gross manners. Even toward my wife . . ."

"Is that as far as it went?"

"I prefer not to dwell on that. . . . There may have been more to it. . . . You saw that sketch he made of her with a few bold brush strokes. . . .

"One overriding passion is enough for any man, Chief Superintendent. . . . I should have stuck to paintings, and kept my collector's fever within reasonable bounds. . . . But it was my misfortune that I happened to meet Mirella. . . . And yet none of this is her fault. . . . What were we talking about?

"Oh, yes . . . who was it who discovered that we were being watched? . . . It was a woman—I can't even remember her name—a stripteaser in a night club on the Champs-Elysées, I think, whom Lucia had brought to the house for Palestri. . . .

"The next day, she called Lucia and told him that, on leaving my house, she had been followed by an odd little man who had accosted her and asked her all sorts of questions. . . . Lucia and Stan kept a lookout, and discovered that there was a skinny, shabbily dressed little man who made a habit of roaming up and down Avenue Junot at night. . . .

"Some days later, they saw him go into the building opposite, in the company of a young girl. . . . He used to sit up there in the dark by the window. . . . He thought no one could see him, but, since he was a compulsive smoker, the glowing tip of his cigarette was visible from time to time. . . ."

"Did it never occur to anyone that he might have been a policeman?"

"Stan Hobson said that if it had been a police operation, the man would have been relieved at intervals, whereas in this case, there was only the one man, which convinced Stan that he must be a member of a rival gang, on the lookout for evidence that could be used to blackmail us. . . .

"It was becoming a matter of urgency to get Palestri out of the house. . . . Lucia and Hobson undertook to arrange it, using Gollan's car. . . ."

"Gollan was in the know, I take it?"

"Palestri refused to go. He was convinced that, having made use of him for the best part of a year, we now intended to eliminate him. . . . There was no choice but to bash him over the head. . . . Not, however, in time to prevent him from throwing his shoes out into the garden. . ."

"Were you present?"

"No."

"And your wife?"·

"No! We were waiting for him to go, so that we could tidy up the studio and his bedroom. . . . Stan had already removed the painting he was working on, the night before. . . . One thing I can assure you, if I have not forfeited the right to ask you to believe me, I knew nothing whatever of their intention to shoot the inspector. . . . It wasn't until I heard the shots that I realized . . ."

There followed a long silence. Maigret was weary, and looked with helpless compassion at the old man facing him as he hesitantly stretched out his hand toward the bottle of brandy.

"May I?"

Having drained the glass, Jonker gave a forced smile.

"In any event, it's all over for me, isn't it? I wonder what I shall miss most. . . ."

His pictures, which had cost him so dear? His wife, about whom he had never had any illusions, but whom he needed so much?

"You'll see, Chief Superintendent, no one will ever believe that an intelligent man could have been so naïve. . . ."

He added, after a moment's reflection:

"Except perhaps another collector . . ."

In another office, Lucas had begun interrogating Bald Stan.

For the next two hours there was much coming and going from one room to another, and a great many questions and answers, accompanied by the chatter of typewriters.

As on the previous night, it was nearly one in the morning before the lights were switched off.

"I'll take you home, mademoiselle. . . . Tonight you will be able to sleep without fear in your own bed. . . ."

They were sitting together in the back of a taxi.

"Are you angry with me, Monsieur Maigret?"

"Why should I be?"

"If I hadn't lost my head and run away, it would have made things a lot easier for you, wouldn't it?"

"We might have cleared up the case a little sooner, but it wouldn't have made any difference to the outcome. . . ."

He seemed none too happy with the outcome, however, and was even prepared to spare a not unsympathetic glance for Mirella as she was led away to the cells.

A month later, Lognon was discharged from the hospital, thinner than ever, but with a gleam in his eye, because he was now something of a hero to his colleagues in the Eighteenth Arrondissement. Better still, it was not Maigret's picture, but his, that had been featured in all the newspapers.

That same day, he and his wife left for a village in the Ardennes, where they stayed for the two months of his convalescence, as ordered by his doctors.

He spent most of those two months, as Madame Maigret had foreseen, dancing attendance on Madame Lognon.

Mario de Lucia had been arrested at the Belgian frontier. He and Hobson were both sentenced to ten years' hard labor.

Gollan denied all knowledge of the attempted murder on Avenue Junot, and got off lightly with a mere two-year sentence for fraud.

Jonker, sentenced to only one year's imprisonment, left the court a free man, having been in custody for six months while awaiting trial, which, according to French law, corresponded to a year's detention after sentence.

Mirella, having been acquitted for want of evidence, went with him, clinging to his arm.

Maigret, who had been standing at the back of the courtroom, was one of the first to leave, to avoid meeting them face to face, and also because he had promised to call Madame Maigret as soon as the verdict was announced.

The trial caused little stir. It was already stale news, and besides, it took place in June, a time of the year when no one talks of anything but where they are going on holiday.

Noland
June 23, 1963